Temperatures are rising...

For Navy SEAL Tye Callahan, Strong, California is a debt of honor and temporary detour in his military career. He's fought hard in Afghanistan and he won't stop until the battle is won. When an ambush he should have prevented kills one of his teammates, however, Tye steps up and steps in to fill the fallen man's obligations. One summer in Strong fighting fires with the smoke jumper team. One fiancée to look out for and get back on her feet. But the adrenaline rush of fighting fire, of jumping into the heart of the flames and pitting wits and body against the inferno, is nothing compared to the rush of coming face to face with Katie Lawson...

Until there's no beating the heat

Katie can't accept her larger-than-life fiancé has been killed in action. While she waits for him to come home, she vows to fulfill his bucket list. And who better to help her than Mr. Tall, Dark and Sexy—her fiancé's teammate and substitute smoke jumper? Now, as the summer heats up one sexy task at a time, they must decide if the chemistry burning between them might just be their second chance at living their own lives... together.

Smoking Hot

ANNE MARSH

Copyright © 2014   Anne Marsh

A All rights reserved. No part of this book may be reproduced or transmitted in any form or by any electronic or mechanical means, including photocopying, recording or by any information storage or retrieval system, with the written permission of the author, except where permitted by law.

ISBN: 0-9910974-5-9

ISBN-13: 978-0-9910974-5-6

Look for these contemporary titles by Anne Marsh

The Hotshots

REBURN
HOT ZONE
FIRED UP

Smoke Jumpers

BURNING UP
SLOW BURN
BURNS SO BAD
SMOKING HOT
SWEET BURN

Dawson Brothers

ONE HOT COWBOY

Harlequin Blaze

WICKED SEXY
WICKED NIGHTS

CHAPTER ONE

Tye Callahan's base camp for the summer was an old camper he'd picked up for two hundred bucks on Craigslist. He'd fumigated his new acquisition, trying hard not to think about any less-than-wholesome activities that might have taken place on the worn-out bed. The camper was a cheap, handy place to crash and that was precisely what he needed. No fuss, no muss. His truck had a hitch too, so he could pull out of town any day of the week. *Could*, not *would*, but the possibility was there. In the meantime, he made do with his own personal fire pit, two Wal-Mart folding chairs, and a solar-heated shower. His new digs were definitely not the Ritz, but the first and last time he'd been inside a five-star hotel, he'd been running a Spec Ops mission, gunning for a suspected terrorist.

This was far better.

His temporary residence in Strong, California involved far fewer bullets and way more logistics—as did his current mission. He hoped. Moving silently, he got his first visual of the firehouse. The town's firefighters had slapped a coat of bright red paint on the outside, but the place was old and fixing it up was still a work in progress. Paint was a good start, though, the first coat glossy enough to see his reflection in. Nothing new there. Aviator sunglasses hid his eyes. The military haircut was still the same, as was the pair of worn BDUs and his favorite—okay, his *only*—pair of steel-toes. The T-shirt was new, navy blue cotton with *Donovan Smoke Jumpers* printed across the front in neat block letters. New job. New threads.

He didn't look like a killer, which just proved that looks were deceiving.

The firehouse door was propped wide open, so there was nothing stopping his forward advance. Intel said his target was indeed inside the building. *Painting.* He'd spent his first three days in Strong learning the lay of the land, where the exit points were. Katherine Lawson rented a bungalow on Spruce Street—and he must be getting used to the wholesome Americana feel of the place because the fact that all the side streets in Strong were named after trees barely made him wince now—and she drove an impossibly small Kia with a correspondingly large dent in the front fender. Surrounded by friends and family, she had plenty of bolt holes if he scared her and she ran.

So he wouldn't scare her.

That's an order, sailor.

He paused just inside the door, quartering the hallway. No visible hostiles, but the open door to his left led out to the garage bays. One fire truck was partially visible, the bay echoing with the cheerful din of men checking gear. Framed black-and-white photographs of the firehouse in its glory days lined the hallway to his right. The place had looked better fifty years ago, no surprise. He'd looked better ten years ago himself. A strong smell of paint wafted from his right and... *bingo.*

Target acquired.

He moved out. The hall went straight for twenty feet, then bent ninety degrees. As soon as he reached the turn, he got his back to the wall. Going in blind wasn't an option he favored, so he peered around the corner and—holy Mary. Targets in the good old U.S. of A. were a hell of a lot prettier than anyone he'd made in Baghdad or Afghanistan.

When the blonde at the bar had mentioned painting, he'd imagined a gallon of Behr's finest and some roller action. Color him wrong. His target faced off against a large wall half-filled with an explosion of pinks, greens and yellows, although he had no idea what the mess was supposed to be. She fisted a paintbrush like it was a weapon, reaching out to brush another stroke of bright pink over the layers and layers of paint on the wall, her ponytail bouncing as she worked. The shoulder-length hair was mostly brown, but the southernmost end was pink and—he squinted—purple. *Huh.* He hadn't spotted any purple in the monstrosity she'd splattered on the wall.

She brandished the brush at the wall. "You, sir, are supposed to be done."

Tye looked at the wall again. Nope. The wall still sported a good fifteen square feet of empty space. Unless this was some kind of post-modernist crap, she was way behind schedule.

She sighed, cursed—was that *French?*—and bent over to dunk her brush in the paint can by her bare feet.

Color him a dirty old man because, sweet Jesus, in all his thirty-two years he'd never seen a sexier pair of legs. Katherine Lawson—and if this woman wasn't Katherine, he'd eat his BDUs—wore some kind of itty-bitty romper thing where the top and the bottom were all one piece. One very short, ass-hugging, boob-clinging piece covered with yellow and white polka dots and held up by thin straps. A lacy scrap of ribbon traced her cleavage and outlined sweet curves his fingers itched to touch. Hiding a bra underneath that top was mission impossible, which had to be his favorite part of her get-up. If he dipped his fingers beneath the edge, he'd find nothing but sweet, bare skin.

Stand down, sailor.

This was Kade's girl? The letters she'd written Kade had been funny, although not half as funny as the wicked drawings she'd doodled in the margins. Little vignettes from Strong, poking gentle fun at the town's residents and small town life. Reassuringly, blessedly normal news and chitchat while he and Kade had been parked in the middle of hell. He hadn't realized how young she was. Kade had been twenty-eight to Tye's thirty-two, but Kade's Katherine... was even younger. No wonder Kade had worried about her. Had made Tye promise to look after her if shit hit the fan and he couldn't finish the job.

As she crouched to daub more paint on the bottom of the mural-in-progress, Tye reminded himself he wasn't on leave. The romper pulled tight, outlining the curve of her ass and hinting at a tantalizing strip of hot pink that definitely advertised thong territory. He wasn't here to—*Jesus*—date or even one-night-stand Katherine Lawson. There was one reason and one reason only for his presence in Strong. To make sure she was as okay as she could be. He had to do whatever he could to make up for his part in her fiancé's death and that dose of cold reality took care of whatever else might have been stirring in his BDUs.

Almost.

Except then... the firehouse siren went off. With a startled shriek—Katherine Lawson had a pair of lungs on her, because he heard her over the siren's ear-splitting wail—she toppled backward. Tye sprang into action, swiftly closing the gap between them to crouch down behind her and cup her elbows.

Her head rocked backwards, banging into his chest even as her back hit his spread thighs. He caught a glimpse of wide brown eyes before she twisted in his arms. Yup. He'd scared the shit out of her. *Way to go.*

Her foot lashed out and the paint can flew up. An Olympic diver would have scored full marks for the perfect somersault—and then lost every last point on the ultimate splat. He'd had no idea one small can could contain that much paint. There was paint on the wall, on the floor, and all over those long, bare legs he'd be fantasizing about later tonight... He tightened his fingers on her elbows, holding her above the rapidly spreading pool of pink.

"I've got this," she snapped, jerking against his hold. "Let go."

No, she didn't.

But, hey, he knew *no* when he heard it and he was turning over a new, gentlemanly leaf. So he let go and she ass-planted right in the small lake of paint. Right at his feet.

"That's what I was trying to avoid," he observed.

"*Merde*," she said with the worst French accent he'd ever heard and tried to get to her feet.

He could see what was coming next, but there was no way he moved in time. She slipped—the paint was as slippery as it was colorful—and her hands shot out, grabbing for support. Her palm slapped against his crotch, painting his BDUs with a hot pink X-marks-the-spot.

"Oh, my God." She stared at her hand like she couldn't believe she'd just pawed a total stranger. Which meant she also stared right at his dick, which decided her words had to be a compliment. "I mean, *mon dieu.*"

He grinned as parts of him shot to life. She yanked her fingers away.

Merde, merde, merde. Katie scrambled backwards from the large, dominating male looking her over. Even crouching, his steel-toes planted on the worn linoleum, he wasn't eye-level with her. And, oh God, she'd touched his goodies. His really, really impressive goodies. Maybe the floor would give way and take her with it. Or she'd wake up and this would be one of those dreams where she was strolling down Main

Street in her laundry day undies while every hot guy in town stared, and not in a good way.

She closed her eyes.

When she opened her eyes, he'd be gone. Or this would be just a dream.

His rough, raspy voice sounded close to her ear. "Katherine Lawson?"

She cracked an eye. He was staring at her like she was crazy. And he knew her name. So maybe he wasn't a random stranger. She didn't know if that was better or worse.

She said the first thing that came to mind. *"Je ne sais pas."*

Time for all those hours listening to her French MP4s to come in handy. She could be the sophisticated, non-English-speaking, soon-to-return-to-Paris exchange student. Anyone, in fact, other than who she was.

He dipped his head, his mouth inching close to her ear. "You're not French. And that's the wrong answer."

Darn it. He sounded certain. "How did you know?"

He crossed his arms over his chest, all stern-looking and in charge. He positively radiated danger and authority, except—her eyes dipped south before she could check herself—for the bright pink handprint decorating his fly. Hard to be Mr. Big, Bad and Dangerous wearing that splash of color.

He didn't look away, but the corner of his mouth quirked up. He didn't seem mortally offended by her assault but, then again, he was a guy. For all she knew, he had a fantasy about getting it on in public in a firehouse.

He leaned toward her, his forearms relaxed on his thighs. He looked like the kind of man who ran ten miles a day in combat boots. Kade had done that. Every morning of their last summer together, she'd sat with her feet up on her porch, waving him on as he ran and catcalling him something fierce because that was what friends *did* and they'd always, always been friends, both before and after they'd gotten engaged. She eyed the BDUs and blinked. She didn't have tears in her eyes. She *didn't*.

"I spent six months in Afghanistan. The French peacekeeping force cursed worse than any SEAL," he said.

"Prove it."

He shrugged and leaned forward until she could feel the warmth of his body, his knees brushing hers. Then he whispered a *really* salty French curse in her ear. At least she thought he did. If she was being honest, her French didn't extend past basic body parts.

He rocked back on his heels. "Convinced?"

"Well, shoot. *Merde*," she corrected. "I'm supposed to be practicing. To get better."

She'd certainly planned on having an entire lifetime—or two or three, if the reincarnation thing turned out to be an option—to learn French. She needed the time because the language-learning gene had clearly skipped her entirely. It was just that learning the language was on Kade's bucket list and she'd made conquering that list her own personal mission. She honestly didn't know why Kade had wanted to learn French—probably because he wanted to go to France, or read a French menu, or impress a girl. Knowing Kade, the answer was all three. Kade was definitely the kind of guy who lived on Santa's naughty list.

Her mystery man shook his head. "I'm going to be cashing a pension check before you get better. Your accent's even worse than Kade's was."

She ignored his use of the past tense. "You know Kade?"

"Yeah. I did." He flowed effortlessly to his feet, paint-free except for that single X-rated spot. How had he managed that? He strode away before she could correct him.

"Do," she bellowed after him, standing up and keeping her feet this time. "Do know Kade."

Just when she thought he'd left her standing there—admittedly, in a mess of her own making, but still—he returned with a fistful of rags. Practical *and* hot. It was her lucky day.

He squatted and wrapped a large hand around her right ankle. "Lift."

Well. Oookay. Mr. Tall, Dark and Deadly clearly had the military training—although the haircut and the dog tags would have given it away. "*Do* know Kade," she repeated.

He shook his head and wiped paint off her foot, carefully setting it down on a piece of paper towel. "He's dead, Katherine."

"Katie." Her embarrassment at pawing the man's crotch (and her second and third glances had confirmed it was still a really, really impressive crotch) was not helped by the fact that he'd decided to play cleanup crew. On the other hand, refusing his help meant either tracking paint down the hallway to the bathroom—which *she'd* then have to clean up—or performing some kind of mutant snail crawl to said lavatory. That kind of thing ended up on Facebook fast.

"Katie, huh?" He flashed her another quick, hard look from eyes that said he'd seen plenty. That just reminded her of Kade again, so she grinned, forcing the dark thoughts back into their box.

Mystery man stared at her dimples, his fingers flexing on the rags. She had no idea what he was thinking, but she took a stab at it anyhow while she waited for the gods to bless her with secret mind-reading powers.

"Switch." He tapped her left ankle with his fingers. The goosebumps were because the rag was cold and not for any other reason.

"Kade's not dead." Sure, she was apparently the only person who believed that, but one person was better than none. Every instinct screamed her fiancé was still alive. Obviously, he'd run into trouble—or he'd be here himself—but he was coming home.

The alternative was unacceptable.

"He is." Her rescuer stood and placed his hands on her waist, swinging her effortlessly over the paint before she could so much as squeak.

"You can't know that."

"Can too. I was there."

"Who are you?" she asked, when what she really meant was *How?*

Reaching over, she nudged his sunglasses up. He let her. That surprised her as much as anything about today because he wore that aura of a leashed predator like other men wore Ray-Bans. He was definitely deadly. Imagining him moving through the back streets of Baghdad with a semi-automatic in front of him was all too easy. The look in his eyes was serious. Hard. The small lines fanning out from the corners could have been due to age. Sun. Experience. Any one or all of those three were possible, but the one thing they sure weren't were laugh lines.

"I served on Kade's SEAL team. Tye Callahan." He stuck out a hand, looked down at hers, and handed her the pile of rags instead.

"Well, Tye Callahan," she said, wiping off the paint the best she could, "I don't believe Kade's dead."

"Uh-huh. I was there," he repeated. "I saw the insurgents surround Kade. We were pinned down, taking some heavy fire. We'd called for backup, but our boys had our position wrong and we got in the way of their insurgent meet-and-greet."

"Really?" He sounded like a late night movie and she must have sounded as confused as she felt because he heaved a sigh and summed up for her.

"Kade got hit by friendly fire. There was nothing left but a crater."

She stared at him. "You redefine *blunt*."

He stared right back, not moving. "You want me to lie to you?"

She had a feeling he would, if that was what she wanted. His dark eyes held hers, making her wonder what else he'd seen. She pushed the wave of sadness away. No matter what Tye Callahan thought he'd seen, Kade was coming home. He was just delayed because he'd never been on time for a damned thing in his life. Believing anything else was impossible.

Taking the rags back from her, he spread her fingers out and began to methodically wipe the paint off.

"You fought with Kade?" Kade had mentioned the guy. What had he said? She racked her brain. Oh, yeah. Big, badass, and deadly. She could see that. Despite that, her libido was jumping up and down, going *Pick me!*

"I did," he agreed, his voice tight with an emotion she couldn't identify.

"And you saw it all."

"Jesus." He balled up the dirty rags. "Sure. It was dark o'clock. Our Humvee hit an IED and we got out, which was dumb luck right there. We were pinned down in a back alley, taking fire from hostiles. Then, our team got into the act and fired. Ten seconds later the insurgents—and Kade—cratered."

"No one told me," she said. "Not the details."

Walking away from an IED was lottery ticket material in itself.

He shrugged. "It's probably classified."

"Why are you here?" She forced herself to step away.

"At the firehouse? Or in Strong?"

Both were good questions. Right then, he'd clearly made it his mission to help her clean up. Or, if she was being honest with herself, he'd taken charge of the mop up operation and she was just along for the ride.

"Either," she said finally.

He nodded. "I promised Kade I'd look out for you. You got shoes?"

Well. Alrighty then. She hadn't seen that one coming, but the request certainly sounded like Kade and right now she'd take any connection to him that she could get.

She motioned towards the corner. "Campers," she said.

He stared. She'd bet he knew the brand name for every handgun out there, so she wasn't taking any guff because she could name her shoemaker.

"Those are shoes?" He sounded slightly stunned.

What was wrong with him? Her shoes weren't just nice—they were spectacular. The canvas shoes had a little curved wooden heel and green ribbons that tied over the instep for those days she needed a little extra jaunty in her step. Plus, not only were they covered in tiny pink roses, but they were comfortable *and* feminine. A double-win.

"They're Spanish."

He looked skeptical. She looked at his feet and, sure enough, he sported a pair of combat boots so shiny she could see her face. Her red and pink face.

"You could buy a small car in some countries for what these shoes cost," she pointed out. He still didn't seem impressed and, really, the price tag wasn't what made the shoes so awesome. That was the wooden heel, in her opinion. She'd spent hours trying to recreate that heel for herself.

"You can walk in those?"

She went for *show* instead of *tell* and slid her feet into the shoes, bracing a hand against his shoulder while she tied the laces. Probably, that touch was playing with fire but she'd already molested the man, so his opinion of her social skills couldn't possibly sink any lower.

As soon as she was shod, he placed her cans and brushes neatly into the milk crate she'd lugged them in with. Apparently, he'd decided painting was done for the day. She snuck a peek at her watch and decided she could live with that. She had an art class to teach at the senior center in an hour and she needed to change first.

Since she was now wearing a quart of pink paint.

"I don't need looking after," she said.

He dropped the dirty rags into the trashcan at the end of the hallway. "Right. Humor me."

"For how long?" Ten minutes, she decided. Humoring him could last that long while he walked her to her car, which she'd driven only because she had what seemed like fifty pounds of art supplies and only two arms. Once they reached the car, she'd pat him on the head—metaphorically speaking, of course, because no one could ever mistake this man for a puppy dog or anything else cuddly or cute—and they'd go their separate ways.

Which was really too bad.

He was the hottest man she'd seen all summer and, given the delicious abundance of firefighters in Strong, that was saying something.

He shoved his sunglasses back into place.

"You've got me for the summer."

He shouldered the door open and held it for her.

Oh, she wished. She really, really wished he were hers.

Instead, he led the way to her car—which wasn't creepy at all, she told herself, because it wasn't like any of Strong's firefighters would even fit in her tiny purple Kia, so it just *had* to be hers—put her things in the backseat, and stood there, hands on his hips and watched her drive off.

CHAPTER TWO

Katie sucked in a deep breath. Think French. And sexy. Millions of people managed this on a daily basis, so why should it be so hard for her? An unexpected image of Tye Callahan popped into her head, all hard muscles, crouched by her feet. Just a tantalizing foot or so from her really good parts.

Even if those parts were drying up from non-use.

She opened her mouth and the syllables rolled out, smooth and sexy and very, very French.

"*Voulez vous coucher avec moi?*"

Commentary was immediate from the woman sprawled in the lime-green plastic Adirondack chair next to Katie. Abbie, the newly-minted Mrs. Donegan and self-styled bestie number two, chewed on her lower lip, clearly trying not to laugh. "I don't think you use *vous* when you're trying to get someone into bed. Unless you're into that whole master-sub thing."

On the other side of Abbie, Laura nodded her head vigorously in agreement. Laura Carpenter might be bestie number one. She covered half the rent check for the bungalow behind them, but she'd never had any problem attracting men.

Maybe neither Laura nor Abbie had never entertained any lovers on a *vous* basis, but God knew Katie didn't excel at that happy flirting thing. It wasn't from lack of trying. Men—well, they tended to pat her on the head and see her as the little sister they'd never known they wanted. That was certainly what Tye Callahan had done. She huffed out a breath. Yep. Kade had said: hey, swing by Strong—which had to be who knew how many miles out of Tye's way—and check on my fiancé... and Tye did. There would be more to the story. Of course, he wouldn't tell her *those* parts, because they'd be dark and gritty, the kinds of things men like him protected the little sister from. Frankly, she was surprised he'd even mentioned how he believed Kade had died.

He hadn't been overly descriptive. She had a feeling getting the man to speak more than a sentence or two would be a feat right up there with running a marathon—which was also on Kade's bucket list, now that she thought about it. She couldn't stop thinking about what Tye had said though. Imagining it was easy. One minute, Tye and Kade had been patrolling and the next... boom. Hostile fire. Friendly fire. Everything all mixed up and gone to hell, until that final explosion rocked her world and Kade was gone.

Temporarily.

Temporarily gone.

As disturbing as Tye's brief account had been, he hadn't seen a body. The Humvee had exploded or otherwise come to an unexpected halt, but he and Kade had both gotten out. Gunfire had followed and the kind of firefight she'd only seen in the movies. She didn't *believe* that Kade had died. She'd been handed a flag and a medal three months ago, but no fiancé. No body. She and Kade had always had a connection and she was sure she'd know if he was dead.

And she was fairly certain he wasn't.

So, while she wrote letters to her Congresswoman and waited for Kade to hurry up and get his ass home so she could yell at him for making her worry and hug him for the next three years or so, she'd picked out a new project. She always did best when she had a project to focus on. She and Kade had swapped bucket lists while he'd been out in the field. Or, rather, she'd badgered him by email for his list until he'd sent her a list he claimed to have written when he was sixteen. He'd signed off with a rather snarky *You going to take care of this for me?* That had been one of the last emails she'd received from him, so, yeah, she *was* going to take care of that list for him. She'd work her way through his wishes and plans and, when she finally finished, he'd be back home where he belonged.

Everything would be fine.

All she had to do was believe.

Abbie snapped her fingers in front of Katie's face. "Earth to Katie. *Attention!*"

Abbie's accent sounded near perfect. Katie had no idea how she did it. It was almost too bad that her friend was happily married to a member of the Big Bear Hotshot team, because Kade would have loved her accent. She suspected that was why he'd put learning French on his bucket list in the first place.

Kade certainly enjoyed dating and anything that gave him a leg up with the females.

She'd teased him that their engagement would crimp his style, but he'd just flicked her on the nose and told her not to worry about it. After all, it wasn't like they were *really* engaged. Even if all of Strong—and apparently most of the military—believed they were. Kade had "popped the question," so to speak, in Mimi's, Strong's one and only bar, when some I'm-just-passing-through asshole had pressed her a little too hard for her number. She was too nice, Kade said. She said *no* and *piss off* and guys heard *yes, please sit down next to me* and *Rip my panties off, please?*

She wasn't nice.

She was an underemployed art teacher with a shoe fetish, for crying out loud. She'd plenty of practice saying *no* and *you'll get it when I get it*, both to the good folks at the student loan offices and to Visa.

But there was no getting around the fact that she hadn't been able to shoot down the guy in the bar and Kade had been worried and shipping out.

"We should totally do it," he'd said.

"Do what?" She'd watched the other guy lurch out of the bar, holding a wad of paper napkins to his nose—she probably should have gotten on Kade's case for popping the guy—and she'd *fully* expected Kade to suggest a concert or a restaurant. Anything but what he'd said next.

"We should get engaged." Picking up her hand, he ignored the sticky patches from the bar, and looked her in the eye. "How about it, Katie Lawson? Will you marry me?"

"You're joking," she'd announced, scanning the bar for cellphone cameras. Kade loved posting stuff on Facebook, the kind of pictures that haunted you in job interviews or you'd been using your parents' computer and you'd forgotten to sign out.

"I don't think I am," he said. "I'd marry you any day of the week and twice on Sunday. Besides, imagine what everyone will say."

He'd grinned. Kade had been a practical joker and this was the best joke of them all.

Kade was her best friend. He'd been her prom date. They'd also been each other's first kiss because that had made the kissing comfortable. Which had, over the years, also led to comfort sex. They were friends with benefits and a cubic zirconia ring she'd picked out on the Home Shopping Network.

Now, everyone thought she was the grieving fiancée, and she? She didn't know what she was, other than alone and more than a little lost.

"Katie?" Laura rubbed a hand over her shoulder, jerking her back to the present. Yeah. No zoning out in the middle of the French lesson.

"I'm here," she said, then corrected herself. "*Je suis...*"

Somewhere. She was somewhere.

Abbie winced, reconfirming Katie's theory that Abbie might actually know a thing or two about French. The problem was Katie herself had absolutely no ear for accents and the self-teaching thing wasn't working out. Maybe she should sign up for French lessons at the local community college, even if it was a two-hour drive each way. She'd definitely have lots of time to listen to her Rosetta Stone CDs.

"I'm trying," she grumbled and snagged the last chocolate croissant from the plate. Maybe the language would rub off while she ate. Or not. Finding French snacks in Strong was proving almost as hard as learning the language. "This is just harder than I expected."

"Hey." Abbie's fingers slapped the empty plate. "I was counting on that croissant."

Laura eyed the empty plate. "I'm pretty sure the two of you ate all the croissants, leaving none for me."

"I brought French fries." Katie waved at the red and yellow box.

"French fries aren't French," Laura complained. "And I'm almost certain McDonald's is a U.S.-owned corporation."

Katie shrugged. "According to Yahoo! Answers, French people eat French fries and snails for snacks. I preferred the carb approach."

"Snails?"

"Be glad Kade didn't have a culinary bucket list."

Laura slid a fry from the box. "Friendship only goes so far," she warned. "Snails are out of bounds."

Like so many things, including talking about what had *really* happened to Kade and the odds of him coming home.

Not going there.

"I think it's time to try another item on Kade's list."

Abbie and Laura stared. "You don't want to wait until you've got the French thing down?"

It was going to take *years* to learn French. Possibly an eternity. She had her suspicions about her language ability or lack thereof. Tye Callahan, on the other hand, had whispered French curse words in her ear with a near pitch-perfect accent. Which figured. The man reeked of competence.

"I think we need to do more than one thing at a time," she said.

"Who's this *we*, kemo sabe?" Abbie grumbled. "That's not my bucket list we're working on."

"You have a bucket list?"

Abbie grinned. "You bet. Will is helping me check items off."

Katie held a hand up. "Don't tell me. Please."

Good for Abbie. Katie was thrilled her best friend had a sexual bucket list. She really was. She just didn't want to hear the details or imagine the part Abbie's new husband, Will, was playing in that particular to-do list. Ever.

"So I'm pretty busy on the bucket list front," Abbie continued. "But thanks for asking."

"One of you guys is going to help me, right? Please?"

"Katie—" Laura sounded torn between amusement and something more pained. "Why do you have to do this? Knocking off the list won't bring Kade back."

"He's not dead." As long as she kept on believing, it would be true.

Laura gave her The Look. Her friend didn't want to contradict her, but the expression on her face made it perfectly clear she believed Katie was engaging in a whole lot of wishful thinking.

"Okay." Abbie bumped her shoulder with her own. "But why do you need to do his bucket list? At least do a list of your own."

"I can't," she said. She didn't know how to explain the way she felt. She just needed to keep that connection to Kade and this was the only way she'd found. As long as she was thinking about him, acting for him, then he was still coming home. Somehow. Some way. Never mind that the U.S. military was convinced otherwise. And, a small part of her admitted, if everyone else did turn out to be right, she'd at least have these few final memories of Kade. She'd also feel better with company. Moral support. Someone to catch her. Take her pick. She just wasn't ready to let go yet and Kade would have had a good laugh at her crazy-ass way of honoring his memory.

He'd always urged her to live more, live louder.

Kade was a larger-than-life guy himself. Not just his physical size—although he was built like a linebacker—but his zest for living. He'd always laughed louder and longer than anyone she knew. He wouldn't have hesitated if he'd had the chance to swim with sharks or fire a machine gun. She'd bet he'd do it all twice, too.

"You really intend to work through Kade's list?"

"I need to," she said and Laura and Abbie nodded. They'd tease her and they'd protest their involuntary enlistment—but they'd help.

"I've only been married for three months," Abbie warned, as if anyone on the porch was unaware of that fact. "I'm not allowed to break anything. Bones or the law."

"Did Will say that?" Laura eyed the empty plate and sighed. "We need more snacks."

Abbie grinned. "He did. He pointed out that our delayed honeymoon would be a whole lot less fun if I were in a full body cast or prison. I think he might go without me."

"Smart man. Although being immobilized has its possibilities. You'd be amazed at the calls we get." As an EMT, Laura had seen her share of sex acts gone awry. She was also an over-sharer.

"Ewww." Katie clapped her hands over her ears in mock horror. "Leave me with some illusions, okay?" She still had nightmares about old Mr. Cochran and the garden hose.

Abbie shook her head. "That's not Laura's M.O. We've got French covered—and Will said to tell you *thank you* for that, by the way—so what's next?"

Katie reached in her bag and pulled out the list. "We don't have to cover the list in numerical order."

Learn to speak French
Have a ménage a trois. *In French*
Own an island
Fly a helicopter
Ride a Segway
Run a marathon
Steer a hot air balloon
Gamble in Las Vegas
Be an extra in a movie
Write a novel
Climb a mountain
Swim with sharks

Fire a machine gun

She tapped the last item and shrugged. "Kade was sixteen when he wrote this."

"Wow," Abbie said, snagging the list. "He had plenty of energy."

"Has," Katie corrected automatically.

"And a death wish." Laura stared at the list. "In my professional opinion, you'd better up your health insurance before you tackle this. Or switch to one of those high deductible plans, because you're going to need a frequent flyer card at the hospital for some of this stuff."

"We've got the French covered," she decided. "Or close enough."

"We can order croissants," Abbie pointed out. "And I can read the French washing instructions on my shirt tag. That doesn't qualify as fluent."

"We get points for effort." So what if Katie wouldn't be mistaken for a native speaker anytime soon?

"Uh-huh." Abbie scanned the list again. "And you're on your own for number two. That's definitely *no fly* territory for me."

"Sixteen-year-old boys." Laura made a face. "We get plenty of calls on them."

"I'll save that one for last." Katie ignored the way her face burned. Given the current state of her dating life, finding one man was a challenge. Finding two brought to mind phrases like *needle in a haystack* and *once in a blue moon*.

"Really?" Abbie stared at her. "You'd do that just because it's on Kade's list? Because that might be taking things a little too far."

Well. Yeah. But Kade was coming home before she got to the end of the list. Almost definitely. Probably. That was her plan and she was sticking to it. So what if she felt a little superstitious about the list? She shrugged.

"What Kade wants…"

"Kade gets." Laura finished with a grin.

"Are you sure?" Abbie looked at her. "Does this really help?"

Abbie didn't add *bring Kade home*, but Katie knew that was only because Abbie honestly believed Kade had already come home. In a box.

"He wanted to do this," she said, hating the way her voice went soft and her eyes misted up. Fake engagement or not, she and Kade had been happy. And, when he'd shipped out, she'd still been content. Life was more exciting with Kade around, and life in Strong would never be mistaken for life on a grand scale but it was comfortable. And happy-making. She liked teaching art even if it qualified her for food stamps and a SNAP card.

"Live your life for you, not for Kade," Laura said.

"Or for any man," chipped in the brand-spanking-new Mrs. Donegan, cheerfully calling the kettle black.

"Got it," she said and, conveniently, the street offered up a well-timed distraction. Tye Callahan, the man himself in the flesh, drove up to the firehouse, parked his truck, and lifted a toolbox out of the truck bed. There was nothing sexier than a guy who was good with his hands, she thought with a sigh. He could be fun. He could be *hers* for a night. Or two. She squinted at him. Maybe seven. Yeah, definitely seven. She had a feeling it would take at least a week to get him out of her system once she'd had a taste of that particular SEAL.

"Now that's a fine looking man." Abbie waved the list in Tye's direction and Katie snatched the paper back. Just before, you know, something crazy happened like the list flying across the street and plastering itself against Tye's face.

"You're married." It had nothing to do with how Abbie was ogling Tye Callahan's butt.

Abbie shrugged. "I'm not blind. Or dead."

Laura grinned wickedly. "*I* wonder what he's doing in Strong—and if he'd be up for a ménage?"

"He served in Kade's unit."

"You've met our new hottie?"

"We ran into each other at the fire station yesterday." *Literally*. Sharing that information was unnecessary, Katie decided. Not that Laura and Abbie wouldn't have a field day with the crotch paint, but she didn't need to relive the memory. Really. Because she was fairly certain the day was permanently etched into her brain cells anyhow.

Abbie was riveted. "You should ask *him* to help you with Kade's list."

Ummm. Yeah. *So* not going there.

"Ask him," Laura demanded. "Do it. You'd have way more fun with him than with us."

"I have to go to class," she announced and shoved off the seat.

Abbie nodded. "Running."

"Yep." Laura pointed a fry at Tye's truck. "The question is: to or from?"

CHAPTER THREE

Infiltrating Katie's art class was a no-brainer. Hell, all Tye had had to do was place a quick call to the V.A. and they'd given him the date, time and a freebie coupon. Under normal circumstances, still-life painting ranked near the bottom of his preferred list of activities. Fruit was for eating and the only painting he did was of targets.

He parked his truck in front of the pink bungalow that housed the V.A. Strong, it seemed, was short on space for art classes. Katie and her students had been shoehorned into the V.A.'s one available room. Close quarters, the guy on the phone had warned, and a definite lack of elbow space.

No worries.

That would make keeping an eye on her easy, right?

It was his fault Kade wasn't coming home. That was the truth, plain and simple. Command could bullshit all they wanted about the reasons that last mission had headed south into fucked-up territory, but Tye had washed out. He'd *failed*. Checking up on Katie Lawson was a drop in the atonement bucket, but he had to start somewhere. Giving her his summer was nowhere near enough.

Plus, he wasn't the SEAL she wanted anyhow.

That honor went to Kade.

He took the steps two at a time, pushed open the front door and got his bearings. Happy chatter floated down the hall from his right. He counted at least two adult females and one adult male, plus the distinct piping whine of a child. Laying in a course for the noise, he moved out.

Target acquired.

The well-used piece of poster board taped to the wall beside the open door announced he was in the right place, so he stuck his head in the door. Katie Lawson was there all right, passing out paint and brushes and chatting up her handful of students. That was all good.

Except she shouldn't be so... sexy.

She had on some kind of white sundress with little straps that crisscrossed her shoulders and wrapped around her breasts, showcasing plenty of sun-kissed skin. Her hair had been pulled up in a sassy ponytail that bounced around her shoulders as she bent over a canvas, pointing something out to one of the female students. Tye wanted to see that hair down, spread around her face. Maybe while he threaded his fingers through the silky strands and kissed her good. Or bad. Behaving himself was getting harder and harder to do. *Houston, we have a problem.*

"Hey, teach," he said, dead-ending in the doorway.

She turned to face him, stepping out from behind the table, and, sure enough, she had another pair of those shoes on. Fuck-me shoes that shot all of his good intentions to hell. Today's number was a pair of curvy pumps with some kind of red-hot bows curlicueing around the heel. Wherever she shopped, it sure wasn't Wal-Mart. He'd never seen shoes like that before.

"Mr. Callahan," she said, propping her hands on her hips. At least, he thought those were her hips beneath the load of gauzy dress. A man could have plenty of fun hauling that fabric up by the handful.

Stand down.

She was Kade Lawson's fiancé.

Off-limits.

And because he couldn't turn all his thoughts off, he asked the question driving him nuts. "How old are you?"

Checking couldn't hurt.

"That's none of your business," she snapped, moving towards him.

He didn't back up. Nope, he let her keep right on coming until she about smashed into him. He liked that too. Shit, he needed to work on his people skills. She glared up at him because Katie Lawson was short, even wearing those fuck-me pumps she liked so much.

"Twenty-four," the old guy parked on the far side of the table hollered. "She had a birthday last month with strawberry cake."

"Personal info is need to know," she shot back. From the way she cranked her volume up, Tye assumed the old guy was deaf, mostly deaf, or getting there fast. "Why are you here?"

That was a good question and one he'd asked himself a dozen times already today. He'd volunteered to take Kade's place with the smoke jumping team. That was one answer. He had two months of leave and a burning desire to be anywhere other than home in San Diego. That was another. But, the God's honest truth was that he didn't know.

He looked around the room. The walls were decorated with construction paper cutouts from local school kids and apparently left over from Veteran's Day. The hand-drawn messages included plenty of lopsided *thank yous* and black sticks spewing orange flames. Once upon a time, he'd been a kid like that, drawing pictures of battles and peppering vets with questions about what it was like, out there in the field. Crayons and imagination were no preparation for real life, no more natural than the mountain of fruit strategically piled in the center of the table.

"Tye?" Katie's voice pulled him back to the business at hand. At least she'd dropped the *Mr.* He scanned the room one more time, taking in the canvasses propped on table-top easels and the two women who had shoehorned their baby strollers along one side of the table, completely blocking the left side of the room. He winced and went with the simplest answer.

"I'm looking out for you."

She poked him in the chest. "You were serious about that?"

Deadly serious.

He snagged her finger, wrapping his hand around it. "I'm always serious."

She waved a hand toward the door. "Off-duty, sailor. I can take care of myself."

Probably, but she didn't have to. She had him. Instead of following her directions, he made for the empty side of the table, picked a seat, and dropped into it.

"I never said you couldn't," he said.

She followed him and stood over him, her skirts brushing his knee. He fought the urge to wrap a hand around the back of her thigh and pull her down onto his lap.

"I'm teaching," she announced. "This is an art class."

"Okay." He crossed his arms over his chest and met her gaze. The metal folding chair poked him in the ass, but damned if he let her know he was uncomfortable. "I'm in."

"You want to paint a still life?" She looked skeptical and he couldn't blame her.

"Can't think of anywhere else I'd rather be." Which was a lie, of course. He could already feel the walls closing in, and there were definitely too many people crammed into the small space, but forty-five minutes of staring at her had to be worth the close quarters.

She shook her head, giving him a look he couldn't interpret before heading to the front of the room to start the class. That apparently took the form of announcing the class fee—ten bucks—and passing a battered basket decorated with red curlicue ribbons that matched her damn shoes. Tye did a quick count when the basket hit him. Most of the class had stiffed her and the old guy's coupon was expired. He opened his mouth to say something—she caught his eye and frowned. So... oookay.

He dropped ten dollars into the basket. He didn't need the V.A.'s coupon. While Katie got going, passing out paints and drawing their attention to the mound of slightly past its prime fruit heaped up in the center of the table, he kicked back and tried to pretend art classes at the V.A. were precisely how he spent his weekday afternoons. Problem was, looking at the old guy daubing orange onto his canvas square, it was all too easy to imagine this being his life fifty years down the road, when he'd finally cashed out. Hanging at the senior center, pretending oranges were an artistic statement when what he was really after was the company.

Hell.

He and the old guy weren't that far apart after all.

By the time her class finished, Katie's nerves were shot. Usually, she'd cram the painting materials back into her stack of milk crates and lug the lot over to the closet the V.A. had loaned her. The two young mothers had been the first to leave—baby number two was showing definite signs of waking up in his stroller and neither woman liked nursing in class—and then Billy's dad had swung by to pick the five year-old up. Mr. Rickerson was dozing in his chair, which was par for the course. Tye, however, showed no signs of leaving.

He'd watched her intently while she went over the proper brushstroke techniques, like she was debriefing him on the best way to defuse a nuclear warhead or clear a terrorist compound. Then she'd passed out the jar of brushes, dropped a load of paint tubes on the table, and stood back as the noise volume in the room shot through the roof. The two new moms chattered away, comparing colic and teething stories while they grabbed paint haphazardly and started daubing away. Mr. Rickerson demanded she read every label because he'd forgotten his glasses. Again. She suspected the eyewear was just an excuse to lean into her and probably stare down her dress but, hey, the man was over ninety and enjoying his afternoon until Tye's death glare had him averting his eyes.

The new moms were easy enough. They just needed an excuse to get out of the house and a place where schlepping a newborn in a baby carriage was okay. Katie was fine with that. She went over brushstrokes with them, encouraging them to go crazy with their colors and enjoying the way the tension leaked out of their shoulders. Painting was therapeutic.

As she'd pointed out to Tye when he hadn't touched his canvas.

"If you want to stay, you paint," she said, using her sternest teacher voice.

One of the new moms giggled and the five-year old wriggled around to stare. She should have insisted that one of Billy's parents stick around with the kid, but she had her suspicions about what his parents were using their forty-five minutes of free time for.

Tye gave her a long, level look. "Is that so?"

She shrugged. "I'm the teacher. That makes me in charge."

"Is that so?" His dark eyes met hers and she wondered what he was thinking. That small grin tugged at the corner of his mouth again.

"You bet." She nudged a tube of paint towards him. "So get cracking."

"Yes ma'am." He gave her a two-fingered salute, before snagging a brush from the nearest jar. He was humoring her. How many times had Kade given her that same look?

Ten minutes before class ended, Billy succumbed to his five-year old instincts and started flinging paint. Before Katie could move in, Tye was already in motion, crouching down beside the kid to whisper something in his ear and redirect him with an apple from the mountain in the middle of the table.

"Hey." Mr. Rickerson shot him a look. "I was painting that."

"Banana," Tye suggested, nudging Katie's afternoon snack towards the vet. "Paint that instead. Sir."

When he flashed the older guy a salute and a grin, something inside her threatened to melt. She wanted to lean into him and kiss him. Drag him down the hallway, find a supply closet, and hole up for the afternoon. She'd known him for—she did the math in her head—less than forty-eight hours and apparently that was all she needed to know that Tye Callahan was bedroom material. And, quite possibly, keeper material.

Merde.

She stared at Tye as the classroom finally emptied out, willing him to haul his fine ass out of the chair and get a move on. The way those BDUs stretched over his thighs should be illegal. The faded seams had her imagining all sorts of delicious possibilities. She still didn't know what he was doing here. He'd fed her that line about watching out for her and he'd certainly done plenty of staring, but she was dead certain he wasn't here for painting lessons, even though he clearly needed help in that department. He'd methodically painted his entire canvas blue and then drawn a red smiley face in the center.

He was art-challenged.

She should ask him out.

Or maybe just jump his bones.

She eyed the table, assessing. Nope. She'd take a mattress over Formica any day.

"We done here?" he asked and her heart sped up just a little at his use of the word *we*. The pronoun didn't mean anything. She knew that. But it suggested a relationship between the two of them that she was happy to fantasize about.

"Until next Tuesday," she agreed. Tye nodded and then began methodically screwing on caps and washing out brushes. Unasked. Usually, she was on her own for cleanup detail. Mr. Rickerson stuck around like he always did. The old guy was lonely and she enjoyed his company. The others, though, always got going, because they had families waiting and things to do. Tye, apparently, didn't.

Today's T-shirt was gray, with not a wrinkle in sight despite the way the cotton stretched over his shoulders. He'd hooked his sunglasses into the neck of his shirt and, when he bent to snag an AWOL brush from underneath the table—Billy's handiwork—she caught a glimpse of metal dog tags.

God.

He was drop-dead gorgeous.

"That was—" he paused. "Interesting."

"Was this your first art class?" she asked.

He looked at her and that small grin tugged at the corner of his mouth once again. "I was five once. This wasn't my first encounter with paint."

"And there was yesterday," she agreed, feeling a blush fire her face. *Way to go, reminding him you molested him.*

"My best painting memory ever." He held up two fingers. "Scout's honor."

"You don't paint a lot."

He shrugged. "I've done my fair share of houses. And targets."

She didn't want to know. "That doesn't count."

He shrugged again. "Paint is paint."

Really? The man needed help. "Then why are you here?"

Ignoring her question, he tucked her jar of clean brushes into the topmost milk crate and lifted the lot. She enjoyed the way the muscles in his arms bunched. So she was shallow. Sue her.

"Where do you want these?"

Right over here on the table. Just shuck the shirt and lie down...

He stared at her. Right. Simple question.

"The closet," she said and led the way so he could stack the crates inside. When he was done, he turned on his heel, hands on his hips, and surveyed the room.

She got the feeling he could give her an itemized inventory.

"You're good to go." He shut the door behind him, but she was blocking his path and, when he turned, he stopped short to avoid body-slamming her. The move pulled the T-shirt tight across his chest.

Yeah. She absolutely was.

She had no idea why she was imagining hot, no-holds barred sex with this guy. She didn't do casual hook-ups. She'd never been interested in picking someone out at a bar and bringing him home for a night. Nope. That was why Kade had gotten himself "engaged" to her in the first place. She was the kind of person who spent twenty minutes agonizing over which chocolate called her name loudest from the box. And then took two anyhow because she couldn't decide. Huh. Which, she guessed, made Kade's ménage idea less far-fetched than she'd believed.

She stepped to the side, but he didn't go anywhere.

Tye Callahan was pretty much an unknown, she reminded herself. Of course, since Jack Donovan had hired him for the jump team, he was also probably not a psychopath. She didn't need to worry that Strong's finest would be fishing her dead body out of a ditch. Plus, he was one of Uncle Sam's boys and Kade had never raised a red flag about Tye's character, morals, or after work behavior. Which meant she could go out with him.

If he wanted to go out with her.

If he wasn't just being polite.

Unfortunately, there was only one way to find out.

"Do you want to have coffee with me?" she blurted out.

"I thought you'd never ask." Mr. Rickerson popped upright in his chair. "Let's go, baby cheeks."

The coffee place was a two-minute walk and driving was unnecessary, even with Mr. Rickerson in tow. Tucked between the art gallery and the general store, Strong's answer to Starbucks was surprisingly popular for a weekday afternoon. Which might have had something to do with the heavenly aroma of coffee beans and the even more decadent scent of brownies. Fresh, hot brownies. She eyed the case. She had jeans to fit into. Eating anything that full of sugar and butter was definitely out of the question.

Tye parked Mr. Rickerson at a table and then proceeded to order for the three of them. He came back holding out two brownies. One for her and one for—yup—Mr. Rickerson.

"I shouldn't."

He jiggled the paper bag. "I saw you looking."

"Looking is calorie-free."

"Uh-huh." He put a brownie down in front of Mr. Rickerson. "And you look just fine to me."

He grinned at her as he handed over her triple caramel mocha. Hypocritical, but the brownie was the tipping point in her battle to button her jeans. "You go for sugar, don't you?"

Since that was true, she settled for mouthing *thank you* and taking the cup. Of course her SEAL was black coffee, no cream or sugar in sight. While Tye helped

Mr. Rickerson get started on the brownie, Katie fixed his coffee. Ostensibly black, but she knew the drill. Mr. Rickerson took six sugars and two inches of half-and-half. His cup was practically albino when she finished.

Two slurps later and bingo, he was down for his afternoon *siesta* and Katie had worked her way through the better part of the brownie.

"So." Tye looked at her. "Coffee. Is this a get-to-know-you chat or did you have an ulterior motive?"

"Maybe I invite all my new students out," she suggested.

"Maybe." He didn't sound convinced.

"You're the guy who said he was watching out for me," she countered.

"True." He eyed her over the edge of his coffee. "And I am."

He radiated confidence. Competence. He was just what the doctor ordered—and he'd all but promised to help her. In for a penny...

"So, Tye, how do you feel about swimming with sharks?"

Not what he'd been expecting her to say. He had a definite opinion on sharks however, and since she'd asked...

"Been there, done that. Dropped into the Indian Ocean once and those suckers were huge. Definitely a *once was enough* scenario."

That particular insertion had been hairy enough, even without the threat of great whites lurking in the water. He'd seen the shadow right before he jumped from the Blackhawk. Fortunately, the beast had moved on by the time Tye's boots hit the water. Then, they'd just had to contend with taking over a ship full of Malinese pirates.

Katie looked disappointed. "Oh."

"Something you wanted to try?" he drawled, enjoying the way she doodled on a napkin with a pen she'd fished out of her handbag. Little shark fins sprouted around his napkin self.

She tried again. "Running a marathon?"

Clearly, she had an agenda. He eyed her. She was curvy and toned but no marathon runner as far as he could tell. "Uncle Sam's sent me on plenty. You have plans?"

"Yes." She sucked in a breath, crumpling the napkin drawing. Kade had always said she drew when she was thinking or nervous. He wondered which one she was today. And, hell, he'd never figured in any of her doodles before and, yeah, part of him had envied Kade his starring role. He reached out and took the napkin before she could jam it into the now-empty brownie bag. So what if he wanted a souvenir?

"Hit me," he suggested, casually tucking the napkin into his back pocket.

"You know how Kade is," she said, staring at him like a *Who Wants To Be A Millionaire* player down to her final lifeline.

Was, he wanted to say to her, but he'd done enough damage already. He wasn't going to disillusion her, not over coffee and brownies. So he nodded and waited for her to continue.

"And I know most everyone thinks he's not coming home."

"But?" He could absolutely hear the *but*.

"But I think he is. I *believe* he is. He sent me an email right before he disappeared."

"What kind of an email?" He racked his brain, trying to remember if Kade had spilled any details. Mentioned anything important.

She blushed slightly. "A bucket list. He made a list of all the things he wanted to do before he died."

He didn't make lists of things he wanted to do tomorrow or the day after. In his line of work, tomorrow was a dicey proposition and time could run out all too fast. If there was something he wanted to do, he did it.

He eyed the woman sitting across from him.

Right now, he wanted Katie Lawson. In his arms. In his bed. Hell he'd take her sprawled across the coffee shop table, and that was one hell of an image.

"I'm going to do everything on that list," she announced.

Then blushed. What the hell was on that list?

"You going to show me?"

She chewed her lower lip and dove back into the brownie bag. He recognized a deflection when he saw it.

When she'd chewed, swallowed and run out of brownie, she answered his question with one of her own. "You want to do it with me?"

Well. *Yeah.*

She blushed. "That didn't come out right, did it?"

"Depends on what you're offering."

He wished like hell sex was on the menu. He'd sweep her off her feet, carry her out of this coffee shop right now if that was what she was really offering. The pink painting her cheeks, however, said he was going home alone again tonight.

"The bucket list," she enunciated. "Do you want to help me check the remaining stuff off?"

"So that would be a *no* to having sex?" He set his coffee cup down on the table. Jesus, making her blush was fun. Her whole face was on fire now.

She waved a hand. "Sex isn't first on Kade's list."

"You sure your fiancé was a SEAL?"

He shouldn't tease her. On the other hand—his eyes narrowed—what *exactly* was on that list? Because it sure sounded to him like sex might actually *be* on it. Near the bottom, maybe, but that sounded like Kade alright.

"Positive." She leaned towards him. "Will you help me with this?"

"Would swimming with sharks and running a marathon figure on this hypothetical list?"

She smiled. Sweetly. Which was definitely his first warning. "You bet. Kade put some good things on there. Are you in?"

He held out a hand. "I want to see the list."

"I don't have it with me."

He recognized a lie when he heard one. "Bring it."

"Later." She stood up, clearly having decided on a strategic retreat. Since he really wasn't ready to let her go, he shot out a hand and captured her wrist in his fingers. Katie Lawson had the softest skin, even if her pulse beat a get-out-of-Dodge rhythm. Busting her was fine and he had all the time in the world for the next two months. He stroked his thumb over the pale veins and considered his next move.

"Do you mind?" she asked, tugging on her wrist. "I'm attached."

"Katie." He pitched his voice low. "You know I'm going to see that list, right?"

She made a face, which was undoubtedly shorthand for *over my dead body*.

Which was another thing that wasn't happening.

Ever.

She tugged again and he held on for a three count before releasing her. "Tomorrow, we're running."

Grabbing a fresh napkin, she scribbled a time and place. No drawing, though, and that was strangely disappointing.

"Can't wait," he drawled. Watching her swish her way out of the coffee shop, he couldn't help but wonder what she'd wear to run.

Beside him, Mr. Rickerson snorted, waking up. He'd drive the old guy home. Make sure he got in safe and sound.

Mr. Rickerson's gaze followed Tye's. "That's a mighty fine woman."

The old guy slurped his cooling coffee and stared after Katie Lawson.

He wasn't wrong, either. Katie Lawson was one of a kind.

CHAPTER FOUR

Tye braced in the open doorway. The California mountains unfolded three thousand feet beneath his boots, a familiar green and gold patchwork of trees and grassy slopes. Today's mission was no high altitude free fall over the unforgiving Afghani countryside. Those jumps had been pure adrenaline rush, his head shutting down and his training and body taking over until he hit the target, hit the ground.

Overhead, the chopper's rotors beat a steady whup-whup-whup as Spotted Dick leveled them out over the day's jump zone. While this was just a practice run, the team treated it as seriously as the real deal. There was no room for error in the air, and a wildland fire was, in the end, simply one more battlefield. Sure, Mother Nature was lobbing the grenades, but she could be a tough, unforgiving bitch, permitting no ceasefire or retreat.

"You good to go?" Jack Donovan roared the question into Tye's ear. The helmet couldn't block the bellow, nor could the thundering rush of air from the open bay.

Tye flashed a thumbs up. "Fuck yeah."

This was his fourth practice jump with the team. He liked the guys, appreciated the tight camaraderie of the team. The Donovans ran a sharp operation—and a safe one. Jack wouldn't drop him in the field until he was damned sure Tye was ready for it. Tye had been the new guy on plenty of teams before—the SEALs were legendary for their razzing of newbies—and he got it. He had to prove himself. He had to earn his spot.

He grinned fiercely.

That worked for him. As any of his drill instructors could have told Jack, Tye didn't know the meaning of the word *can't*. He'd always had the resolve. Once he decided to do something, he stuck. He *did*. He did *not* quit or ring the bell. So what the hell had happened in Khost?

No. That was definite *no fly* territory there.

That had been three months ago. Uncle Sam had shipped him home for two months of leave and... here he was. In Strong. He'd fielded the calls from home, asking when he was headed San Diego way, and he'd put them off. He didn't deserve to go home. That was the truth.

Jumping out of planes was familiar territory.

Katie Lawson... was not.

"Good man." Jack slapped him on the back and nodded toward the open bay. "Appreciate you stepping in for Kade."

Jesus.

It was the least he could do.

He focused on the small splash of red waiting for him in the meadow sixteen hundred feet below.

Memories shifted in his head, his past clamoring for attention. Other reasons for red. He didn't want to remember. He really, really didn't.

Jack's hard slap on his shoulder, the signal to go, was a welcome disruption.

With a heartfelt *hooyah*, he bailed, launching himself out into the air in the mother of all swan dives, boots up, head down. For a moment, with the wind roaring in his ears and all that open space beneath him, he was at peace with nothing to do but breathe and fall. Zero to one twenty in seconds.

Automatically, he scanned the area around the L.Z., searching the landing zone for insurgent positions and anti-aircraft guns. The air was positively balmy, compared to the frigid temps of his usual HAHO jumpers. Of course, that might have had something to do with the jump altitude. SEALs went airborne at fifteen thousand feet, while the smoke jumpers generally jumped at two to three thousand feet. This time, it was okay for the men on the ground to see him coming. In fact, the California mountains were downright peaceful and hostile-free. No mortars, insurgents or evil-assed camels.

No Kade either.

He got right-side up, feet pointed toward the ground and head in the sky.

Jump thousand.

Look thousand.

Reach thousand. He wrapped his hand around the rip cord, ready to pull.

Wait thousand.

Pull thousand. He yanked hard, the chute flaring open behind him and dragging him briefly back up into the sky.

Check your canopy. Jack's voice echoed in his head, walking him through the safety chant. Staying safe was good. Keeping others safe was better. When he looked up, he was in business, the lines straight and tangle-free as the canopy did its part to arrest his free fall. Seconds later, his boots hit, the impact reverberating up his legs and through his spine almost as hard as the one truth he couldn't out-jump or out-run.

No matter how long he jumped or where, the truth was both simple and inescapable. Kade wasn't coming home.

When Tye showed up, Katie was already running. Or, rather, huffing and puffing her way along the trail Gia Jackson had recommended. A nice, easy loop, the jump team's only female member had promised. *Right.* Yoga had *not* prepared her for this kind of cardio and buying an exercise-appropriate wardrobe online—damn those pop-up ads anyhow—hadn't helped. Even the excuse to buy new shoes wasn't helping.

One mile down and far too many to go.

This was clearly a bucket list, once-in-a-lifetime activity because anyone who actually succeeded in running a marathon undoubtedly planned on dying immediately after he finished it. Sucking in air, she eyed the horizon and the puff of darkish smoke floating over the mountain. The Strong jump team would be busy soon. She hadn't heard the plane go up this morning, though, so she figured her pseudo-date with Tye was still on.

She rounded the bend on the path and considered taking five. Or ten, twenty or thirty. How did the jump team do it? Panting, she skidded to a halt, resting her hands on her thighs. She was fairly certain that was her heart she heard banging over the beat on her iPod.

"You're cheating." The familiar raspy voice behind her had her jumping. Warm fingers tugged her ear buds down. *Tye.*

"If I have a heart attack, I'm blaming you."

It was positively unfair how good he looked in the now-familiar BDUs. He wore a Navy SEALs T-shirt and—of course—the familiar pair of steel-toes. Her heart gave a suspicious thump. *Bad heart.*

He grinned. "Start running."

"I already ran," she groused, but put her feet back in motion. "How long is a marathon?" Maybe she had her facts wrong. Please God.

"Twenty-six miles." He sounded positively cheerful. "Reconsidering?"

"I already signed up for my first marathon." First and last, but she'd keep that tidbit to herself.

"Huh," he said, which she decided to interpret as *Please tell me more, I'm fascinated.*

"Bay to Breakers." Impossibly, the trail headed uphill, making her calves burn with each new step. She made a mental note to check out the marathon course on Google Maps. San Francisco had a reputation for hills.

"That's not a marathon. That's a fucking parade with sneakers." Tye didn't sound like the trail's sudden upward twist posed any kind of problem for him. She considered stopping—she already knew that the Bay to Breakers often walked part or all of the course—but then she'd be tempted to lie down. For the next two, three or forty hours. Just until she caught her breath.

"I heard they wear *costumes*." The look of acute discomfort on Tye's face was an unexpected bonus. "You can run with me. We'll be a team."

"I'm not a Barbie doll you can play dress up with," he warned.

She knew that.

"So," he said when they'd covered the first fifty yards and she'd hit her stride. "You and Kade."

The toe of her sneaker caught on the trail, but Tye was right there, his hand cupping her elbow.

Show no fear. Kade had drummed that into her. "What about us?"

He shook his head. He wasn't even winded, damn him. He made running look effortless which, she reflected, it might be for him. Mr. Big Bad-Ass SEAL probably ran fifty miles a day pulling a semi-truck behind him. The trail headed uphill and she bit back a groan, making a mental note to kill Gia later. Tye would be pushing her in another minute.

"He didn't talk much about having a fiancée," Tye said.

"Probably not." Since she had a feeling the military frowned on practical jokes involving legal status. Not that she and Kade had really been planning on getting married. It was more that they hadn't not planned on it.

Tye made a choked noise. Or bit back a curse. She wasn't sure which, so she risked sliding a glance his way just to know what she was working with here. Not because she enjoyed looking at him. His jaw was tense, his fists clenched. He didn't break his stride, though. She'd give him that.

"That doesn't bother you?" he bit the words out incredulously. "His not mentioning your engagement?"

"Why should it?" This time, she tripped over an invisible rock and he sighed, steadying her.

"Because you were his fiancée, not a dirty little secret."

"Oh." Damn it. Were they climbing a mountain here? The path kept going up and the stitch in her side was about to cut her in half. Gia's idea of easy was clearly suicidal.

"We have an open arrangement," she said as airily as she could, given the marked lack of oxygen in her lungs.

"Katie." Her name was half-groan, half-curse. And wasn't that the story of her life? "If you'd been my fiancée, the whole damn unit would have known. He read parts of your letters out loud. Your drawings were fucking genius."

She opened her mouth and then decided breathing was her priority right now. She sucked in air, panting shallowly. "Okay," she wheezed.

"Deep breaths," he said. The sure command in his voice did something to her insides. And lower.

Definitely lower. "Breathe slow and deep. Keep your shoulders down and breathe from your stomach. Didn't Kade ever take you running?"

Thinking about Kade was the last thing she wanted to do. Tye's big hand pressed against her stomach. Darn it. She'd skipped her sit-ups for the last twelve months or so. And now that it was already bikini season, what was the point? By the point she gave up and admitted that six-pack abs were not in her future, it would be fall and cover up time again.

"Like that yoga thing girls do," he continued, moving his hand away as he slowed his pace to match hers.

She tried and he was right. Breathing did get easier.

"Better?" Yep. One hundred percent self-satisfied male.

"Better doesn't mean good."

"You're the one determined to run a marathon," he pointed out. "I'm just trying to help."

Kade would have done the same thing, although he probably would have smacked her on the ass for good measure and then taken her out for ice cream afterwards. Tears pricked her eyes.

She was such a fake. From the fake engagement to the all-too-real break-up via Skype. She hadn't told anyone in Strong about that particular conversation with Kade. He'd said he wanted her to get out there and look for a real man. He was real. Real enough, at any rate.

"Jesus. Don't cry."

"I'm not." How inelegant would it be if she used the hem of her T-shirt as a Kleenex?

Tye made a noise of disbelief as the one-mile marker flashed by. His skin glistened in the morning sun and she'd bet he hadn't started back at the picnic tables. He pulled off his shirt and stuffed it into her hands.

"Blow," he demanded, like he wasn't running half-naked. Maybe it was a SEAL thing. Or a man thing. "Wipe. Take your pick."

She looked over at him and just about crashed. Tye definitely had six-pack abs. Holy. Moley. Did he ever.

"I'm not using your shirt as a Kleenex," she snapped. She hadn't had that kind of offer since Benjamin Dare had brought her a frog in the second grade. Sweet with a side of really, really gross.

The problem was, she suddenly couldn't see the trail. Because there were tears in her eyes. She sniffed. Not elegantly, either. Nope. She went all out with a loud snort. Tye laughed.

So screw it.

She wiped her eyes and nose on his shirt. She had a feeling the shirt had seen worse.

"Better?"

Not really. She had no idea how her life had ended up like this. Kade was her best friend and now he was gone.

"I'm sorry he's not coming home."

She was proud of herself. She didn't stumble. "He's coming home."

It took willpower to get those three words out.

"Katie—"

"He's not dead," she said fiercely. "I won't let him be. It doesn't feel like he's dead in here."

She thumped her chest with the hand holding Tye's T-shirt. She felt like she was waving a flag, but she wasn't giving in on this one. "I write every week," she said fiercely. "I call. I email. I'm pretty sure half of Washington thinks I'm crazy, while the other half just wants me to go away, but I'm not letting go of this. I'm not letting go of Kade."

There was a pause while he processed that, broken only by the thud of her feet hitting the dirt because, go figure, Tye ran like some kind of lethal Ninja warrior.

"Okay," he said finally. "Let's say Kade's not dead. Then what now?"

She didn't know. She really, really didn't. And that was the problem, wasn't it? Letter writing, emails, even running a marathon… none of that would get Kade home any faster. All it meant was that she didn't forget him and she had a funny feeling that was important.

She shrugged.

"I don't know," she admitted. "But I'm not stopping. Somehow, I'm bringing him home and, until then, I'm going to work my way through his damn bucket list."

They hit the two-mile marker. Thank God. He'd keep on running.

She'd stay put.

It was the story of her life.

Katie had crying and breathing all mixed up. *Jesus.* Tye needed to fix this, fix her, but what did he know about relationships? He was definitely a relationship virgin, having spent his adult life avoiding emotional commitments. Being a Navy SEAL meant shipping out for months at a time—and staying mum about what had happened during the deployment when he was home. Girlfriends and wives didn't like the intel blackout and he couldn't blame them. *That's need-to-know* wasn't the desired response to *How was your trip, honey?*

"I'm done," she announced, coming to a halt. She'd done two miles, which was one and a half miles further than he'd expected. He should have known better than to underestimate her, however. She'd get it done if she'd made up her mind. If there were any way to bring back the dead, Katie would find it. Kade had been a lucky bastard to have her in his life and Tye was pretty sure his friend had known that too.

She dropped onto the bench attached to the picnic table. The spot was less park and more gravel pullout from the highway cutting through the mountains with a few bonus picnic tables. The view, however, was something else again. From the air, freefalling towards the ground, the California mountains were spectacular, all steep peaks and rugged slopes. Plenty of summer color, too, and the sky was a bright pop of blue that could have come from one of those paint tubes she'd passed out in class. He usually preferred to be airborne or at least moving fast and hard, but the view here wasn't bad either.

The mountains were different from those in Afghanistan. Those slopes were hard and unforgiving, all rock and no plant life but sporting plenty of snow and thin air. Beautiful in their own way, but harder and starker. Plus, the locals there weren't exactly friendly. More than one had tried to kill him. Sharing space with Katie was far better, even if his reasons for being here weren't so great. He owed her. It was his fault Kade wasn't coming home and he should front with her about that fuck-up of his, but... he liked spending time with her and she didn't seem to mind his company. He didn't want to lose that.

But she was crying and damned if he knew what his next move should be. He eyed her carefully, like she was a grenade with a hairpin trigger, and she stared back at him, face flushed, eyes damp. She looked wiped and not from the run, either.

She dropped her gaze to his shirt. "I should wash this."

"I've got a spare in my truck. No worries."

"Okay." She chewed on her lower lip like she had plenty more to say but no idea how to get started. A bead of sweat trickled down the vee of her T-shirt and he pretended he wasn't following the trail with heated interest. God was definitely getting even with him.

Deflect.

"You need to stretch." *Jesus.* His voice sounded gruff, like he was some kind of scratchy-voiced late-night DJ.

Taking the shirt from her—his shirt had seen worse than a few tears—he tossed it on the table. "Come on."

He held out his hand and waggled his fingers. She hesitated, then slapped her hand into his and let him pull her to her feet. If she'd been a new recruit, he'd have barked for her to drop and give him twenty. He was all too clear, however, that she wasn't one of his men.

"I thought exercise was supposed to make me feel better," she grumbled. "Or at least shrink my ass."

She looked down at said ass and, like clockwork, his eyes followed. Shit. That wasn't supposed to happen, but her black cotton shorts hugged every curve and, when she twisted, she flashed him a hot pink thong with little flowers. He kept his mouth shut and someone owed him another medal for that.

"Stretch," he repeated, his mouth dry.

"You were a drill sergeant, weren't you?" She eyed him suspiciously.

"I'm telling, not asking." He pointed to the ground. "So get busy."

"I'm pretty certain no one died and made you God." Then she looked horrified because, yeah, she'd just alluded to the elephant in the proverbial room. Kade being dead was on the *do not discuss* list. Please God don't let her cry, he mentally begged whatever higher power might be listening. He didn't deserve the intervention, but she definitely didn't deserve the pain.

"It's going to be okay," he said gruffly.

"How do you know?"

He didn't and that was the problem, wasn't it? "Whatever I can do, it's yours."

"Thanks," she said softly. Interpreting the look on her face was impossible, so he gave up trying.

Instead, he slapped a hand on the edge of the table and concentrated on pulling his right knee up behind him, stretching out his quad. Before he did something stupid like, say, yank her into his arms and hold onto her.

With a sigh, she hopped up onto the table and did some complicated bendy thing with her right leg bent in front of her and her left leg stretched behind her, sinking into the pose with a groan. *Jesus.* That sound should be illegal. Instead of taking pity on him, though, she arched her back, pressing down on her hands until her breasts pointed sky-high, taking his gaze with them.

She caught him looking, which wasn't hard since her tabletop deal put her right on eye level with him. "Not SEAL standard?"

He shook his head, not sure he'd get the words out. "One word. *Yoga.*"

He'd heard of it. He'd just never *seen* it up close and personal. Yoga was as foreign to his world as MREs and mortar rounds were to hers. But, Jesus Christ, Katie was flexible. His mind immediately headed down all sorts of dirty pathways.

"You should try it," she said.

He didn't know what he would have said—probably a *hell, no*—but a truck backfired and his day went to shit. Not a gun. Not ordnance. Just a truck that was somewhere too close—the parking lot, the last rational bit of his mind supplied—and a short, sharp bark of sound echoed off the mountainsides and punched through his head. A truck backfiring. Logically, he knew that.

His heart didn't get the memo though.

Nor did his pulse.

Or his lungs.

Nope, his body kicked into full overdrive, hurtling him towards memory lane and Khost's too narrow, too familiar city streets. God. Damn. It. Heart pounding overtime, lungs seizing, he dropped to the ground, knowing there was no way he could avert the panic attack.

CHAPTER FIVE

Tye had dreamed about Afghanistan last night, and those dreams refused to go away like the doctor had ordered now the sun was up. Nope, the Technicolor dreams haunted him, filled with plenty of blood, screaming and random body parts he was almost certain didn't belong to him. It was hard to tell sometimes when he was asleep and when he was awake. He'd led plenty of missions as a SEAL, and he didn't relive any of those ops when his head hit the pillow.

Fuck. He was fucked up. Broken. And none of that was acceptable. He was supposed to be strong. How the hell could he take care of Katie when he couldn't even take care of himself?

Kade wouldn't have broken down like this.

"Tye?" Katie's voice reached him from somewhere nearby. "Are you okay?"

Nope. Not by a long shot, but he'd rather cut off an arm—and possibly both legs—before he admitted as much. *He* was supposed to take care of *her*.

Which made her the last person he wanted seeing his sorry self right now.

"Fine," he gritted out.

He gave in to the weakness and buried his face in the crook of his arm for one second. Memories shifted, overlaying each other until he didn't know what was real and what his head had embellished. All he knew was that he hated it, hated the helpless feeling. Usually, running helped. Run enough miles and he sometimes outran the demons. Now, since Katie clearly wasn't ready for a ten-mile run, his only option was endless reps of push-ups. Up, then down. Faster and faster, because maybe the burn of his muscles could drive away these memories.

From somewhere close by, the sound of bare feet reached him. When he turned his head, he could see her toes out of the corner of his eyes. She'd kicked off her sneakers, revealing pretty green polish.

Get it together.

"You're not okay," Katie stated from overhead.

Yeah. Newsflash. Something had broken in him on that last tour, and he had no idea how to fix it. He grunted and started a muscle-searing set of reps. Maybe she'd take the hint and leave. No one in his unit stuck around when he got in one of his moods. He wanted Katie gone. Now. Especially since he had a bad feeling she recognized exactly what was happening to him.

He dropped onto the grass, sweat dripping off his forehead, and set his mental clock for ten seconds.

"I'm busy here," he ground out.

"Exercising?" She didn't sound like she believed him. Her voice rose. "Some more? What happened to stretching and cool down?"

"Yeah. Change of plans." He shoved up and started the next set of reps. "So go away."

She considered his words for a moment. "I'm not interested in going away."

Warmth and amusement filled her voice. Sympathy was missing, though, for which he was pathetically grateful.

"Definitely exercise," he ground out. "Highly recommended."

"If you say so." To his surprise, she dropped down next to him. "Maybe I should give it a shot." She did, although her form was wrong. She had her ass in the air, and she'd be sorer than shit tomorrow.

"Suit yourself." He wondered how long she'd last. For the next two minutes, they did push-ups together. He outpaced her five to one, but her company was strangely comforting.

"Jesus," she ground out, and the name sure sounded like a prayer to him. Her arms trembled. "How do you do this?"

The smile tugging at his lips surprised even him. "Practice. Whereas you, clearly, have been slacking."

She shot him a sideways glare. "I work out. You ran with me today."

Yeah. He had. He shot her a look and waited.

She flopped onto her stomach, cradling her forehead on her arms. "Do you do this every day?"

"Pretty much." Especially when the memories came back with a vengeance. Two more reps was his usual prescription. Then it would be safe to stop. Her presence next to him was different, but he liked it. There were better ways to get her all hot and bothered—much better ways, certain parts of his anatomy reminded him—but this was unexpectedly fun. He certainly couldn't remember any time his PTSD had ended with laughter.

"That's brutal," she complained, but the smile was still on her face.

At least he could show her how to do a proper push-up.

"Get up," he said and switched to a one-handed push-up, using his free hand to swat her ass. She had a great ass.

"Hey." She turned her head and eyed him. "Keep the kinky stuff to yourself."

He grinned, unable to stop himself. "You'd like it. Remember, you've got a bucket list to check off."

"Yeah. Promises." She flopped her head back down on her arms.

"Up," he ordered. "You're doing it all wrong."

Yeah. That was definitely feminine outrage sparkling in her eyes when she turned her head to mock glare at him. Good. She'd pushed his buttons, so getting a little of his own back seemed only fair. And fun.

"We are still talking about push-ups, right?"

"Absolutely," he assured her. Squatting beside her, he rearranged her arms and legs into the proper push-up form. He was pretty sure that was a muttered curse he heard.

"I'm an expert at push-ups." It felt good to tease her. "Five and a half days of training in BUD/S Hell Week alone," he continued. "We did push-ups holding a damn log over our heads. This is nothing. Drop and give me five."

"Or?" She turned her head and grinned at him, braced on her arms. He swept an arm down her back and legs. Just to check her form, he assured himself. And because he'd really enjoyed swatting her ass.

"You need motivation?" He leaned forward, arms on his thighs. His mouth brushed the sensitive skin near her ear.

"Yes." She sounded breathless. He didn't know if that was because of the push-ups—or him. He'd rather it was him, though, so he leaned in closer still. Nipped her ear as he tapped her ass again. Not hard. Just enough, though, that she sucked in her breath.

"I think you'd like my kink just fine," he said. "Drop and give me five."

He was half-surprised when she did. His hand guided her up and down, keeping her ass in place and her line straight.

"Okay," she gasped out. "I believe you."

"About the kink?"

"About the exercise," she said firmly. "Although if you require this level of effort from all your partners, I'm making a mental note not to interrupt any exercising you do in the future."

"Don't make promises you can't keep."

Grinning, he got to his feet and held out a hand. She took it, curling her fingers around his. That felt right too, as did the way she shot up off the ground and into his arms.

"I'll make you a deal." Katie tilted her back and eyed her companion. Tye hadn't changed in the last ten minutes. Nope, he was still a big, bad-ass SEAL. Any other time she wouldn't have complained. Hell, she would have been all over him. But he was hurting, even if it apparently would kill him to admit the truth. Kade would have done the same.

She didn't want to leave him like this. Didn't want to pretend that everything was fine—*normal*—when it so very clearly was not. Tye needed fixing. She wasn't entirely sure what she could do, but someone needed to do something.

And she was here.

And she *wanted* to do something...

Him, if she was being honest. Which she could be to herself. That was okay. The words never had to cross her lips. Plus, she was fairly certain Tye was in no condition to be starting any kind of a relationship. She'd read up on PTSD as soon as Kade had shipped out because unfortunately too many of the military's finest came home and had to face their demons. Over and over. The fierce look on Tye's face as he drove his body up and down in a vicious set of gut-wrenching pushups? Yeah. She wasn't a doctor, but she knew a problem when she saw him.

And she still wanted him.

She wasn't sure what that said about her, but she admired his tenacity and his refusal to give into whatever horrific messages his brain was telegraphing him. He'd worked it out, although she'd never realized a body could do that literally.

"What kind of a deal?" He let go of her fingers like he suddenly realized he was hanging on. Reaching out, she snagged his hand. *She* wasn't ready to let go yet.

"I'm an art therapist."

Three, two, one and—yep—cue the look of frozen horror on Tye's face.

"Wow," he said. "I thought you painted. Murals and stuff. And taught those classes at the veterans' center."

"I do." It wasn't all that hard to interpret the new expression on his face. Now he was wondering if she'd correctly connected the dots and realized he was having some kind of flashback or PTSD attack. Followed by the realization that she absolutely had and now she wanted to *fix* him. In her experience with guys, none of them admitted to having problems or needing solutions. They preferred to pretend that everything was just fine.

He was precisely the same.

Okay. Scratch that. In this one instance, he was as pigheaded and stubborn as every other male of her acquaintance. In every other particular, he was stunningly, deliciously different. She groaned and he raised a brow.

"Problems in the art world?"

He had no idea.

"Art can be very therapeutic," she tried again. "Painting's a great way to exorcise demons or work through dreams."

"I had no idea those were therapy bananas yesterday." His shuttered expression still said he disagreed with her statement one hundred percent.

She decided not to elbow him.

"So I'll trade you. I'll give you art lessons in exchange for your help with my bucket list."

"Right. The bucket list you won't let me see. You need to stretch more," he called after her. "Or you're going to be sorer than shit tomorrow."

She turned and marched back to her car. She'd never admit that the muscles of her ass were *already* sore from their run. She popped the door and eyed the devastation of her front passenger seat. She should probably excavate the car at some point.

"You should lock that." Now he sounded faintly incredulous. Which was, she decided, better than closed down or defensive. Even if it was at her expense.

"We're in the middle of nowhere." If she wasn't safe here, where was she safe?

He moved closer, a big, heated body she could feel at her back. Her hormones jumped up and down with glee, since this was the closest they'd been to an attractive man in—she counted—two years.

"You have no idea who you could run into out here," he pointed out. His mouth brushed her ear. She wished the accidental caress had lasted longer, because her arousal shouldn't go zero to sixty from such a small thing.

"In Strong? Please." Her voice didn't shake. It really, really didn't.

Much.

"How long is this bucket list?" he asked suspiciously. His fingers cupped her jaw, the touch so light that she could almost pretend it wasn't happening.

He was thinking about it. Squashing a smile, she leaned in and grabbed her tote bag from beneath a stack of design notebooks.

"Jesus," he groaned. "Please tell me your wallet isn't in there."

She shrugged. So she wouldn't tell him.

"I'll make you that deal," she said instead. She turned around, back to the car door and grinned up at him.

No kissing Kade's fiancée. That had to be rule number one.

But her smile warmed him up in places he hadn't known were still numb after the bone-chilling cold of mountain nights in Afghanistan, something all the gear in the world couldn't cure because the problem went so much deeper than the thermometer. Katie looked at him and a smile tugged at the corners of her mouth, had dimples digging into her cheeks. She'd have smile lines by the time she was forty, wearing all that happiness on her face. She'd be even more beautiful then than she was now.

"You have a deal for me." Talking had to be safer than kissing.

"You help me. In exchange, I give you art lessons."

He didn't want to paint. Apparently, though, what he wanted didn't matter here.

Which he knew already, because for no particular reason, he wanted Katie. Wanted her just because she was Katie.

"Well?" she prompted, when he didn't jump on her offer.

He wondered if she usually had many takers for free art lessons. Probably too many, given the state of her Kia. She needed a job with a paycheck.

"You don't need to pay me." After all, he owed her, even if she didn't know it.

She gave him what he was coming to think of as The Look. Kade hadn't mentioned The Look when he'd talked about Katie, but the man had clearly omitted several key details. Like how stubborn and feisty and determined to do things her way Katie was. And—he glanced in the backseat of her car—the crazy shoe fetish. He'd bet she needed a closet just for her footwear. The backseat held a whole heap of heels in a rainbow of colors.

"I like to be square," she said. "If you're going to do this, I want to do something for you."

He could think of all sorts of things she could do for him, starting with running her lips down his neck. "I'm not a cheap date."

"Art lessons don't come cheap."

She'd decided to give him the hard sell. He bit back a grin. He'd played poker almost nightly with a dozen of the most bad-ass SEALs around. She wasn't out-negotiating him.

"I charge ten dollars a lesson and that's the group fee. It's more for private sessions."

Deflection time. He snagged the bag from her and dropped it on the trunk. "Is the list in here?"

She laughed. No more tears—he'd done something right. "Tye—"

Hearing her laugh was worth everything. Moving swiftly, he popped the snap and shook it open. The inside of her bag was even worse than the backseat of her car. Not only did the bag weigh a good fifteen pounds, but it clearly doubled as a second closet. Or a trash can. He wasn't really sure which.

"That's mine." Her hand reached around him, feeling for the bag. "Give it back."

"Nuh-uh." He shook the contents. "I'm going in and you owe me hazard pay."

"Don't malign my bag." She ducked under his arm, but that move left her sandwiched between him and the Kia's trunk. Not a whole lot of space, he thought happily, as her backside pressed against his front, making parts of him stand to attention. "That's Coach."

"You name your bag?" He'd named dogs. His unit had adopted an Afghan dog, feeding the animal, watching out for him, and generally loving on him whenever a damp nose nudged their hands. Or their guns, boots, or packs. Stan, so named because of the plethora of Waziristans, Nuristans, and other places ending in -stan on the Afghan map. *Kade* had wanted to bring the dog home.

Katie's finger jabbed the hot pink circle on the bag's side. *Coach.* Apparently, that was a brand name. And a good one, too, based on her exasperated huff. He'd know next time. Methodically, he rifled through the contents. Which consisted of completely disorganized layers of crap interspersed with various female bits and pieces. *Jesus.* And a strip of condoms.

"I want to see that list."

"Need-to-know," she chirped.

"You made me curious," he argued, pretending he hadn't just manhandled her condom stash. "And I think I should know what I'm getting into. There's a reason why you're offering to trade these high-priced art lessons for my services. I'd like to know what it is."

"Well, I didn't think you'd take a pair of heels," she said. "Although I can certainly switch the offer up if you'd prefer shoes."

"No shoes," he agreed.

"You knew Kade. I think he would have liked this."

Kade would have kicked his ass six ways to Sunday and back for what Tye was thinking.

He filtered another layer of crap, more cautiously this time, and came up with some kind of bright blue leather slipper thing curling up on itself. He had no idea where someone would wear a shoe like that. At least, he thought it was a shoe. Maybe. And then there it was—an eight by fourteen piece of yellow notepad paper folded into thick eighths like some kind of grade school love note. *Bingo.* He plucked the list out of her bag.

She made a sound like a distressed bird and twisted in his arms until she faced him, reaching up for the note that he held out of her reach. Which wasn't hard because Katie wasn't an overachiever in the height department.

He waved the paper, shaking out the folds. "Let's see what we've got."

"That's private." She leaned into him, stretching. Apparently, full body contact wasn't off-limits in her rule book.

"Not for long," he grinned at her and started scanning. "I'm not sure you should be allowed near a machine gun."

"Says you," she grumbled, reaching half-heartedly for the list again.

He gently batted her hand away. "Sharks. A mountain. And an entire novel. Are you sure this list is Kade's? The man bitched about completing a postcard."

"He wrote to me."

He didn't want to think about that, so he went on reading. When he got to the top of the list, he knew precisely what Katie hadn't wanted him to see. He raised a brow. "You've got your work cut out for you. And I think you need to recruit another girl if you're planning on a proper ménage."

And there it was—her blush. He'd hit pay dirt all right. "That's Kade's list."

He shrugged. "You're the one who said she planned on checking the items off his bucket list. Every. Single. One."

Face still pink, she got back in the game, raising a brow. "I can find another guy."

And... point to her, because his reaction to the mere thought of *sharing* Katie with any one was off the radar. "Since this is Kade's list, you need to find a girl."

"You wish," she groused.

She had no idea how badly he *wished*. "Uh-huh. Count me in."

CHAPTER SIX

"When are you coming home?" Tye's father sounded the same as ever. "Your mother and me, we'd like to know. We'll make some plans."

Hell.

The family phone call probably shouldn't make Tye feel like he had his back to the wall and his weapon up, only to discover that the clip had jammed. Going home for the summer hadn't been part of his plans. He had Kade's temporary gig in Strong to fulfill and the man's fiancée to sort. In other words, his plate was full.

You don't want to go home, a little voice said.

He ignored it.

"Not this leave," he said, because clearly once hadn't been enough.

"You've got two months, right?" His father circled back to the meat of the problem like a shark scenting chum.

"I've got plans." Cradling his cell phone between his ear and his shoulder, he moved to the RV's kitchen counter and grabbed the loaf of bread he'd bought in town. Maybe carbs would help. "I signed on for the summer with the Strong smoke jumping team."

"Sure," his dad acknowledged, tiptoeing around the elephant in the room. They both knew Tye was supposed to be taking time off—not moonlighting as a smoke jumper. "But you get time off, right? There's no reason why you can't come down for a weekend."

And there it was. The *son, I'm disappointed in you* tone that made Tye feel like he was twelve again. He slapped peanut butter on whole wheat while he considered his answer. He didn't miss the MREs, but his own cooking wasn't much of a step up. Thank God for the camp cooks.

"One weekend," his dad said, twisting the parental screws just a little tighter. "For your mom. You do what you need to do the other seven, but give her those two days."

Tye didn't wash out or ring the bell. He'd survived the hell that was BUD/S training and not once had he been tempted to cross the deck and ring the bell that signaled he was quitting. Instead, he'd rolled with the challenges. Beaten them. *Won.* But, Jesus, the rulebook didn't apply to parents.

"I'll see what I can do," he said, meaning *Please let me hang up the phone.*

"Tye—" His dad huffed out a breath. "You were overseas for ten months. Your mother misses you. I miss you. So level with me. Why can't you come home?"

"I have something I need to do here."

"And it has to take all summer?"

Maybe. Hell, he didn't know. How long did it take a woman to get over her fiancée's death and get her own life back on track? Katie's face as she ran had been determined but teary, as spunky as those ridiculous shoes of hers. She wouldn't let life knock her down for long.

"I lost a man," he said, instead of answering his father's question. "In Afghanistan. His fiancée lives here in Strong."

"You can't live his life for him," his dad pointed out. "If that's what you were thinking of doing."

"I know that." He stared out the RV's open door. A couple of smoke jumpers wandered by, headed for their own temporary shack-ups. Several guys were also batching it in trailers for the summer, while others camped up in the row of rental cabins near the hangar. The place buzzed with easy camaraderie and there were plenty of pizza dinners when camp food got old, followed by a cold beer for the off-duty. It was like summer camp for adults, in some ways, except that when the call came in, these guys would go up and out the plane bay, determined to fight whatever wildland fire needed fighting.

He understood why Kade Jordan had wanted to come back here. This fight made a hell of a lot more sense than the fights in Afghanistan or the Middle East, where the SEALs had only a piece of the intel picture.

"Look. Maybe we can come up, okay?" his dad offered.

"I don't know when I'll be on the ground." Fire was unpredictable. "But that would be great."

Not.

He wasn't ready to talk about what had happened in Afghanistan and his parents would ask. That was the thing about love: it worried. His mother would want to fix him and his father would get behind her one hundred and ten percent. Dealing with all that concern was just not something he could do right now. So here he was. In Strong.

And... he spotted incoming.

Katie Lawson pulled up in front of his RV, precisely fourteen minutes late. Frankly, he was amazed that itty-bitty, too-purple Kia had managed highway speeds. He eyeballed the car, but the sides and fenders seemed good. She hadn't acquired any more dings since the last time he'd seen her.

"I have to go," he said.

While his father worked his way through the goodbye spiel, Tye watched Katie extricate herself from the car. His eyes went straight to her shoes and he could feel himself smiling. Kade hadn't mentioned the thing she had for ridiculously feminine shoes. Maybe it was a new thing and the other man hadn't known.

He liked that even better, pretending he had a piece of Katie that had been off-limits to Kade.

"You're starting with an easy one." Hands on her hips, Katie pouted at him. Deliberately. He recognized the look. She'd play him for all she was worth and then she'd reel him in. The catch would be sweet, but he'd be dancing to her tune. Had it worked on Kade?

"I told you before, no machine guns." He tapped the end of her nose. "It's Segway or nothing today."

He'd borrowed the Segway from a local police unit where a former SEAL team member was working and the x2 looked pretty bad-ass with oversized treaded tires and plenty of black. There was also an add-on bumper, so no worries if she dumped the Patroller.

Joey, however, looked like he might not let go of the fender frame. He'd volunteered to help Tye unload the Patroller from the back of Tye's pickup and Tye was fairly certain it was lust on first sight on Joey's part.

"That's a sweet ride. Are you keeping it all summer?" Yeah. That was naked longing in the other jumper's voice.

"Long enough," he said. "You can ride it later."

The *get lost* was plenty clear in his voice. Katie got the first ride, no matter how many covetous looks the other smoke jumpers tossed her way. He'd share his toys later. Joey finally ambled off with one last lustful look at the Segway and Katie watched him go.

"He could have taken it out for a spin."

"Ladies first."

She shot him a grin. "Joey would tell you I'm no lady."

He wasn't stupid. He wasn't answering that. "So, sharks, huh?" he deflected.

Her smile lit him up inside and made him want to do whatever it took to earn a repeat. Huh. He ran through a few quick memories, but he couldn't remember ever feeling like that before. He'd earned winning times on a course. Medals. And kill counts. Smiles, however, were foreign territory.

She ran a finger down the handlebar. "I like fish. I love the ocean."

Uninvited, his imagination immediately transplanted her into the middle of the Indian Ocean. Surrounded by fifteen-foot sharks. He didn't think that was what she had in mind. Of course, his next mental image—of her in a shark cage with the toothy bastards swimming around her and knocking into the bars—wasn't much better. Cage diving was safer than what the SEALs got up to, but it was also no afternoon snorkel with stingrays. Fortunately, there were plenty of other items on Kade's bucket list.

And ecoparks. He was fairly certain there was at least one ecopark in Mexico where you wadded into a pen up to your knees and, boom, there were the sharks. That might be safe enough, plus he'd get to see her in a bikini.

"Swimming with sharks is pretty hard to do when you're landlocked."

"I'm up for a field trip."

"Not today," he said, because he wasn't. He had commitments to the jump team and he wasn't ready to leave Strong anyhow. Being in Strong felt right, the place strangely peaceful, with a side of smoking hot. Both literally and figuratively, he thought, running his gaze over Katie.

"Do I pass inspection?"

And...there was another land mine and a question with no right answer. Her white sundress was going to drive him crazy long before they finished the ride. The dress was made out of some kind of floaty fabric with thin ribbons crisscrossing her shoulders. Little white buttons marched down the front, making him wonder if they were decorative—or functional. Flicking them open one by one would be the best kind of Christmas present.

The shoes, however, were a different kind of problem.

She stuck out a foot for said inspection, presenting a red leather boot with appliqués of white moons and yellow stars. More buttons marched up the side. Apparently, Katie had a thing for buttons. Unfortunately, the sexy heel was only part of the problem. The boots also stopped two inches south of her knees. Her dress started three north of her knees. He wanted to wrap his hands around her bare legs and explore.

"You can't ride in those boots," he decided. "You'll fall off."

She eyed the Segway's platform. "I've been standing for years, Tye. I'm not going to fall off."

While she stared at the Segway, he stared at her legs. Falling off was the least of his worries. She was Kade's fiancée, for Christ's sake. He had no business looking at her and imagining those red boots wrapped around his waist, the heels digging into the small of his back as he took her on a very different kind of ride. The problem was, he couldn't seem to turn off the fantasies where Katie was concerned.

"Show me how to ride this thing," she ordered and parts of him—southern, unruly parts—wanted to do just that.

"Don't you own a pair of sneakers?"

She turned her head and looked at him. Laughter crinkled the corner of her eyes. "Don't you own anything besides those steel-toes?"

"What's wrong with my boots?"

"You own just one pair of shoes. That's it, isn't it?"

He had a pair of hiking boots. And he was fairly certain he also had a pair of sneakers. Somewhere.

"Two," he said. "I own two pairs of shoes. Possibly three, but I'd need to confirm the whereabouts of the third."

She stepped closer, the frothy material of her skirt brushing his thighs. "That's seriously sub-standard."

"What do I need more for?" He narrowed his eyes. "How many pairs do you have?"

And why had he noticed her shoes anyhow? Because they demanded attention, he decided virtuously.

She waved a hand. "I honestly have no idea."

"Guess."

She chewed on her lower lip, clearly considering a resounding *no*.

"Or I'm not letting you on the Segway," he said. "Joey can have the first ride after all."

"All of my shoes?" she asked. "Or just the ones I made?"

"You make your own shoes?" Maybe that explained the collection.

"I made these." She wiggled her foot at him and her skirt spilled back higher. *Jesus.* Both the shoes and the legs were gorgeous.

"I picked mine up from the PX." He shrugged, playing it casual. "They get the job done."

From the pained look on her face, shoes weren't a function in her world. Negative. They were a *calling* along the lines of a religious vocation. He made a mental note not to damage any of her footwear.

"I've always had a thing for shoes." She shrugged. "From the moment I got my first Barbie and realized you could buy cards and cards of these little plastic pumps. Barbie had shoes for every outfit. Learning how to make them was a better way to feed the addiction."

"I thought Barbie was a feminist nightmare."

"She was fun, although the shoes were a killer. I'd pop them on my fingers and walk them around."

O-kay. And he'd been making weapons out of anything he could get his hands on when he was that age.

"Do I get to ride?"

"Yeah," he said, giving in because he was being an ornery bastard and he knew it. It wasn't her fault— much—that her shoes redefined *come fuck me* shoes. His problem. Not hers.

"But let's review the safety protocols and how-tos, okay?"

"*Maraveilleux*," she said and he figured swimming with the sharks was safe because, damn, her French accent needed work. Lots and lots of work. She wasn't checking *learn French* off Kade's bucket list any time soon.

"Shift your weight forward to go straight; lean backward to go backwards; squeeze the handle left or right. It's pretty basic."

"Got it." She hopped onto the platform, clearly itching to get started.

Yeah. Time to rain on her parade somehow. He stepped up behind her, putting his arms around her and covering her hands on the grip.

"Scoot forward," he demanded, pressing against her back. And her legs and her ass... There were advantages to sharing a Segway built for one.

"I thought I got to drive," she groused.

"Not this time," he said, although he'd seen her Kia and the answer was really *not a chance in hell*. He had to return this thing in one piece.

She should get to drive. After all, it was her bucket list—or, rather, Kade's. And Kade was her sort-of fiancé. They slowly moved down the runway, the Segway rolling smoothly over the asphalt as Tye drove like a little old grandma.

"Some speed would be good."

He didn't take his eyes off the runway. "You want to go faster?"

"There's no *faster* about it," she grumbled. "We'd have to actually be going *fast* first."

He chuckled. "You've got a thing for speed, don't you?"

No. She just didn't have a thing for *slow*. Life had a habit of passing by unless she reached out and grabbed it with both hands. She'd learned that the hard way. She eyed the speed setting.

"This is turtle mode."

"Uh-huh," he agreed. "Enjoy the scenery."

The problem was, this scenery was all too familiar. They'd started close to the Donovans' big metal hangar and now they were putting down the runway, past a DC-13 and a chopper. She'd seen these planes before. She'd seen this tarmac. Riding a Segway was supposed to be exciting. Different. Something more than this slow, sedate glide. When they hit the halfway mark on the runway, she wiggled herself into position by his side. She liked doing this better *with* him. Otherwise, it felt too much like he was driving.

Which he was.

Darn alpha male.

She leaned back against Tye, feeling the tension in his hard body. Since she was apparently just along for the glide at the moment, she looked up at his face. And... *merde*. He had his eyes focused on the horizon, a SEAL on a mission. This was supposed to be fun. Kade had always had plenty of fun and lots of laughs. There wasn't a bar where the man wasn't welcome and no one he couldn't win over. Tye looked like he was planning on storming an insurgent stronghold at the end of the runway.

That needed to change. Tye needed to have some fun. She slid her hands out from underneath his and slapped her palms over his fingers. There. Now she had a shot at being in control. "My turn."

He hesitated, his fingers tensing beneath hers. Then he let go. Not happily, she knew, and probably not for long, but she'd take it. She promptly adjusted the speed setting, because this beginning mode wasn't what she wanted. Not, she thought, that "standard" was much better. Apparently the makers of Segway were anti-speed too. There wasn't a "fast," "furious," or "go, baby, go" setting anywhere to be seen. The Segway picked up speed, though, and she'd bet they were going all of twelve miles an hour.

They hit a bump. Okay. She steered them straight through a pothole. That was the truth, plain and simple. Tye's arm snaked around her waist and he cursed. *Not* in French. Nope. She understood what he said perfectly well.

"Eyes on the road," Mr. Grim Reaper demanded in her ear.

"You always play by the rules?"

"When my team's safety is at stake? Absolutely." His jaw tightened and he wrested control of the Segway from him.

"I don't like playing by the rules," she informed him, turning to face him.

"You do today." He steered them left, making a tidy circuit of the landing strip behind the jump hangar. Katie counted two more planes parked on the runway and a half dozen pick-up trucks fanned out in a semi-circle. The place was peaceful and quiet. *Boring.*

Then he stopped fast and that move threw her against his chest, because she hadn't been holding on. Nope. She'd been letting go big time.

She finger walked up his chest. "Penalty on the play."

He eyed her. "That's the worst sports metaphor I've ever heard.""

"Suck it up." She nudged his sunglasses up.

Danger, danger, Will Robinson. Tye had old eyes, like she'd thought the first time she'd seen him, but there was something else there now, something she couldn't help but respond to. *Heat.* For *her*, Katie Lawson. She'd never been a *femme fatale*. Despite her man problem at the bar that had made Kade pony up his faux fiancé services, guys tended to see her as the fun friend. The girl they played with on the softball team and chatted up while they went after girls like Laura and Abbie. Tye, however, looked at her like he could eat her up.

And she liked it.

Which was so, so bad of her.

Instead of turning around or getting off the Segway or doing any one of a dozen practical things, she slid her hands up his arms. His shoulders were as hard and powerful as the rest of him as he brought the Segway to a gentle halt. Good. Causing an accident wasn't on *her* bucket list.

"I've got worse metaphors," she promised and his lips quirked.

"Can't wait for the show-and-tell." He stood there, less than an inch of space between them and that slightly amused look curling his mouth. Her whole body was shrieking *oui, oui, oui* while her head countered with *C'est impossible!*

"First base," she whispered and, when he ducked his head to catch her words, she kissed him. Which was all his fault, she decided. He looked so hungry, what else was she supposed to do?

Her mouth pressed against his, her lips slightly parted so she could catch his lower lip between hers. A soft, sipping kiss, just tasting him the slightest bit because he was probably—okay, definitely—off-limits and at no point had she asked him if this kissing business was okay. But he tasted perfect. She ran her tongue over his bottom lip just to make certain. Yup.

He tasted perfect.

"Katie—" Her name on his lips was part need, but mostly protest.

Tye jumped off the Segway so fast he ass-planted. *Smooth.*

"What the hell was that?"

"A kiss." She glared at him, all *no shit, Sherlock* perched on the borrowed Segway.

"That's not on the list," he accused.

"Having a ménage is." Damned if she didn't look hopeful. Or something. He wasn't sure what that *something* was, but he was in trouble here.

"I can count to three, angel. There are two people here."

He wanted to leap back on that Segway. Or pull her down to the ground with him, get her underneath him and—

He wrestled his rebellious thoughts under control. "I thought you wanted to wait until Kade comes home to tackle the ménage to do."

Right. Kade. He needed to be remembering his man down and not how Katie's breasts had felt pressed up against his own chest.

"You think I'm a nice girl." She hopped off the Segway and crouched beside him, stabbing a finger into his chest accusingly.

Yeah. He did.

"You're wrong."

He really, really wished he were.

She chewed on her lower lip and he wondered if Kade had told her that little gesture was her tell and betrayed her every time she started fudging the truth. "About Kade and I—"

"Save it," he said, standing up. "I don't want to hear the details. Consider that kiss practice, for when Kade comes home."

He wished his return trip to the hangar was a victory march, but the ride was more of a strategic retreat. Katie's belief in Kade's coming home was contagious, it really was, but like catching a killer cold or that H1N1 swine flu. It wasn't healthy. He couldn't afford to think that way.

After all, no one knew better than he did that Kade was gone for good.

CHAPTER SEVEN

The flames licked over the tree canopy, creating a column of smoke visible for miles. Tye knew this, because he had a ringside seat for the fire's next move. The jump team had hunkered down in their safety zone to wait out the fire currently parting around them like the Red Sea. Today's safety zone was a previously-burned area which meant he was pretty much sitting on a pile of charcoal while the flames roared left and right. His present situation made Khost and the Afghan countryside actually look like a safe bet. The team had jumped in yesterday afternoon and then spent the night knocking down the flames. That had been good, hard work. There were no nightmares when he didn't sleep. It was perfect.

A tanker chugged overhead, dropping a load of pink retardant onto the flames. Pink rain, Tye thought. It was an absolute Dr. Seuss moment. Fortunately, today's exit plan didn't involve a pack-out. Instead, the team was waiting for a chopper pick up. Thank God, because Tye didn't see anything remotely resembling either a trail or flat terrain.

"We should have brought hot dogs." Evan Donovan was a big guy, a broad-shouldered man who looked like he played defense for a football team. He was also a man on a mission as he tugged his protective gloves off and dug into an MRE he'd fished out of his pack.

"Do you ever think about anything besides your stomach?" Rio punched his brother in the shoulder in easy camaraderie.

Tye liked the Donovan brothers. They were good guys and all former military.

Evan chewed, then swallowed. "That fire gets any closer and we're going home minus a few parts."

Tye eyeballed the fire, but the Donovans seemed unconcerned. The other jumpers sprawled on their packs, feet up and asses planted. Joey was asleep. *Jesus.* If the Donovans weren't worried, however, Tye was good. Mostly.

"Mandatory break time," Jack said, when Tye raised an eyebrow and looked his way. "Mother nature wants to make sure we get our state-mandated ten minute time out."

"No worries." Tye pushed his helmet back, swiping at his forehead. He was pretty sure he'd just redistributed the black from the ash.

"Good." Jack eyed him. "Sometimes, the new guys worry."

"No idea why." Tye watched the wall of flame sweeping past them. The flames' roar approximated that of a freight train, drowning out the sound of the guys shifting. He took a drink from his canteen. Their picnic spot was uncomfortably hot, but pulling off his

Nomex now was an unacceptable risk. He flexed his gloved hands. Nope. The gloves stayed on. Just in case.

"Be honest. How many team members do you fry?"

"On a yearly basis?" Jack grinned. "Why do you think we had a vacancy for you?"

Tye snorted, then sobered.

Jack clearly knew where Tye's head had gone. "Kade was a good guy. He'll be missed."

He raised his canteen in a silent toast to the flames.

"He was the best." Better than Tye. He should definitely be the one standing here, ass deep in fire.

Jack eyed the flames. "Ten more minutes and we're good to go."

Hefting his Pulaski, Tye mentally laid down his line. "I'm ready whenever you are."

"Have you thought about what you're doing when summer is over?"

Tye eyed him. "Uncle Sam has requested an encore."

"Requesting isn't the same thing as ordering," Jack pointed out. "Re-upping is a choice."

"Not for me. Is that what Kade was shooting for? A permanent berth on the team?"

"This isn't about Kade," Jack said easily, shoving to his feet. "Or what he might have wanted."

But it *was*. Standing up, Tye slapped his helmet back into place. He had Kade's place on the jump team. It wasn't like he hadn't had the best of reasons for volunteering. Hell, he'd known the jump team had been left shorthanded and experienced jumpers weren't so easy to find. He'd been happy to step up and he was enjoying his summer. But he also wanted Kade's fiancée and not for altruistic reasons.

Katie was gorgeous, sexy as hell and, yep, still completely off-limits. That crazy bucket list project? He got it. She wanted to do what Kade would have done. Well, Kade wouldn't have kissed him, Tye knew that for certain. Keeping his hands to himself would be a challenge but he was a Navy SEAL and difficult was his specialty.

"If you change your mind, there's a permanent place for you on the jump team," Jack volunteered. "We could use another good man and you know your way around a plane. Spotted Dick bought himself a place down in Belize."

Tye wasn't a good man.

"Retirement property?" He had no idea how old Spotted Dick was, but the guy had clearly seen more than one firefight. He would have pegged him for the kind of guy who fought until the end though.

"Bone fishing." Jack grinned. "He wants the odd week off here and there. I don't think anyone could get him to pack it in permanently."

Tye could sympathize. Parking his ass on a beach and watching the waves come in and go out seemed like a life sentence of boredom. *Pass.*

"I appreciate the offer." Tye turned to face the fire. The flames looked shorter, right? Not quite as hungry? Jack seemed satisfied, however.

"That's not a *yes.*"

Okay. Jack might be satisfied with the fire's progress, but with this conversation? Not so much.

"Nope." Part of him wished the next word out of his mouth could be that *yes*.

Jack Donovan fell into step beside him and they walked the line together in silence, assessing the fire's progress. Even Tye could see that the flames had stopped their urgent forward movement. There were no obvious breaks or hotspots. The dirt line the jump team had carved inches deep into the topsoil had done the trick. They'd jumped in to get there first—and fast. The Big Bear Rogues would come up the fire roads as far as they could and then pack in. Those hotshots would knock the fire down the rest of the way.

"Think it over," Jack said when they turned to head back to the team. "My offer stands, for the summer at least."

The deafening beat of the chopper coming in overhead made answering unnecessary. The bird descended carefully until it hovered just above the ground, sending a blast of hot, ash-filled air over the group.

"Did someone call a taxi?" Evan roared loud enough to be heard over the chop, motioning for the team to pile in. That sounded good to Tye. Right now, he was jonesing for a hot shower, some food, and his pillow. He helped the guys toss packs through the open bay door, then scrambled aboard, hooking his fingers through the webbing on the wall to lean back out the open door and score a last look at the fire as the pilot took them up and through the pall of smoke, swinging over the mountainside and headed for home. Airborne, they shot through the bright blue of the morning sky.

"We got her contained." Evan high-fived his brother and settled into a yelled recap of the fire's trickier moments.

Opting out of the highlights reel, Will Donegan elbowed Tye. "You got your truck back at base? Can I bum a ride into Strong?"

"No problem." He didn't feel like being alone anyhow. A ride-along in his cab would be welcome. "You didn't drive?"

Below them, the dark green tops of pines poked up out of puffy white smoke. If it hadn't been for the spot fires burning merrily, the scene below could have been one of those Christmas displays with cotton-ball snow.

Will grinned. "My wife has the truck, but she's not driving it home. Sunday morning mimosas with the girlfriends," he explained, when Tye raised a brow. "Good times, but I'll be lucky if she's walking straight."

Tye decided not to weigh in on that one. Ten minutes later and Strong came in sight as the chopper neared the airstrip. *Home.*

Just for the summer, he reminded himself.

Don't get used to it. Don't put down roots. He'd ship out in September and this would all be over.

When Katie got home from church on Sunday morning, Abbie and Laura were already parked on the front porch. They'd had the same Sunday morning ritual for the last four years and nothing—certainly not marriage or men—would change that, they'd promised each other.

"You got the goods?" Laura's gaze went straight to the plastic grocery bag Katie was schlepping.

"You bet."

Every Sunday morning, they toasted the previous week with mimosas after church (or drank their consolation prize, as Laura had pointed out after more than one bad week) and devoured one of those tubes of frozen cinnamon rolls. None of them was much of a cook but Pillsbury rocked their worlds.

Since it was her turn to "cook," Katie headed inside, set the oven and pop-pop-popped the cinnamon rolls onto a cookie sheet. The ETA to delicious gooey goodness was twenty minutes. She eyed the stove. Or maybe she'd give it twenty-three because she was in no mood to wait for the oven to warm up. She shoved the goods into the stone-cold oven, set the timer, and headed back on out to the porch.

"Have a seat." Abbie patted the Adirondack chair to her left. "Tell me that *you* have stories, because Laura here is coming up dry."

That was unusual. Between the highway accidents she cleaned up as an EMT and the shenanigans her fellow EMTs got up to, Laura was usually better than reality T.V.

Laura shrugged. "So everyone drove safe this week and the guys behaved themselves. Unfortunately, it won't last."

Laura passed her a mimosa made from the bottle of sparkling wine—none of them had the budget for the real stuff—parked in a plastic bucket full of ice by her feet. Asking where the bucket had come from was probably unwise, but Katie was almost certain she'd never filled it up with Pine-Sol, so as long as she didn't lick the bottle, she was probably safe. Sometimes Laura took practical to a whole different level.

"So we're counting on you for exciting updates." Abbie made a give-it-up gesture. "Don't disappoint."

"I think I assaulted Tye," she said glumly.

Abbie snorted mimosa out of her nose and Laura tossed her a roll of paper towels.

"Either you did or you didn't." Laura took a swig of her own drink. "There's not too much grey area."

"Are we talking—" Abbie punched the air with her fists. "Or..." She blew an air kiss.

"The latter. The former. *Merde*. How come I can never keep straight which is which? I kissed him."

Abbie and Laura traded looks.

"You don't look surprised."

Tye had, though. Right before he'd really, really gotten into kissing her back—and before he'd removed her mouth from his.

"On a scale of one to ten, how hot was the kiss? What?" Laura asked when Abbie smacked her. "That's relevant information. It leads to the whole *was it an assault or not?* question."

"I have a hard time imagining Tye Callahan being a bad kisser." Abbie grinned. "And I've had a damned good time imagining it."

Laura eyed her. "You know, you really don't act married."

"Again, I'm married, not dead." Abbie shrugged. "Will knows he's the best. When I compare him to others, I appreciate him even more."

"Whatever." Laura shook her head and topped off her plastic flute. "Good thing I'm off duty today because I'm ninety eight percent certain my BAC just passed the legal limit."

"I kissed him," Katie admitted. "So his skills don't really come into it."

Abbie turned to Laura. "How good of a kisser is Katie?"

"Hell if I know." Laura kicked her steel-toes up on the porch railing. "I haven't French-kissed her since we were eleven and curious. And, no, I'm not taking one for the team here and repeating the experiment. Once was enough for me, thank you."

Katie made a face. "I was still better than you."

"Keep saying that." Laura grinned. "But I'm not the one worrying she assaulted a guy."

Given Laura's blunt approach to life, Katie decided, it was kind of surprising it hadn't happened already. Laura had no problem walking straight up to a guy and telling him she found him attractive. Or unattractive, an asshole, or just plain in her way. You always knew exactly where you stood with Laura.

Abbie sighed, clearly abandoning the test plan approach. Thank God. "Did he use the *assault*?"

"I kissed him."

And it was a fairly humiliating memory as far as kissing war stories went. She wouldn't have minded if he'd seemed to enjoy the exercise, but after those first few moments when he'd almost kissed her back, he'd been... frozen. Then he'd all but fallen off the Segway. So, no, that kiss wasn't going in the keeper column as far as memories went.

"Did he kiss you back?"

"Or did he screech like a virgin, yelling *Back the fuck up?*" Laura brightened, clearly enjoying the mental image.

"I thought he was *going* to kiss me back," she emphasized. Didn't men like take-charge women who made the first move? "Then he backed up so fast that he fell over."

"Maybe he wasn't in the mood." Abbie looked thoughtful. Katie appreciated the excuse, but she knew an excuse when she heard one.

"He's a guy." Laura held the bottle out to Katie. "More? Guys are always in the mood."

"Will says that's not true." Since Abbie was the only one of them who was married, that had to give her an edge in the credibility department. Maybe. Or maybe Katie was just desperate to find some understandable, non-personal reason why Tye Callahan had backed the hell off.

"It's true," Abbie insisted, when Laura looked incredulous. "Sometimes, a guy just isn't in the mood. No one's up for sex twenty four/seven."

"The guys on the EMT didn't get that memo. Sex is pretty much all they talk about. That, or grievous bodily injuries and which roads you can get the most speed on." Laura waved her glass. "Will is an anomaly."

Abbie grinned. "I can safely assure you he thinks about sex all the time."

"I don't want to know," Katie groaned. "Can we get back to my problem here before I need more therapy?"

"So you kissed Tye Callahan and he backed off." Abbie shrugged. "Just do it again."

"Do it *right*," Laura added. "Or make sure you've got him pinned against a wall so he can't fall over."

"Bottom line: good move," Abbie said decisively.

"Good?" Maybe Katie and Abbie had different definitions of the word.

"It's time for you to move on, to get over Kade. I know—" Abbie held up a hand. "You're sure he's coming back and I really, really hope you're right but… the odds aren't great, sweetie. Uncle Sam buried him. Your Tye saw it happen. Even if there's no body, I think it's unlikely Kade got out of that particular mess. And he wouldn't want you to sit around and wait for him the next fifty years or so."

"Even less than you think." She sucked in a breath. Confession was good for the soul, right?

"Come again?"

"Kade and I weren't really quite engaged." She let the words hang in the air and busied herself petting her Siamese. Angus liked the attention, stretching out to fill her lap and then some.

"That's kind of like assault," Laura pointed out. "You either do—or you don't."

"Then we didn't. You remember the night he proposed to me at Mimi's bar?"

"Sweetie," Abbie said dryly, "Most of Strong remembers that night at the bar."

"Well, some guy who was passing through had been heckling me. Kade thought I could use an assist, so he stepped in and then he suggested we should get engaged."

"Because he didn't think you could handle drunk assholes on your own?" Laura's brows rose.

"Yes. No. He thought it was funny. And helpful." She added the last bit hastily. Her engagement had been more than just a joke.

"Wow." Abbie blinked. "I didn't see that coming."

Laura snorted. "Yeah. None of us did."

A truck door slammed in the driveway and booted feet pounded towards the porch, startling the cat, who bolted in a show of indignantly fluffed fur. Will Donegan rounded the corner. His hair was damp from a recent shower, but the cleanup had been quick. Ash still streaked his neck and forearms.

"I'm here to collect my wife if you ladies are willing to share." He grinned and took the steps two at a time.

Laura shook her head, laughing. "Firefighters. So hot, but always in a rush. You could just stand there and let me look at you."

"Looking, yes. Touching, no. This one's all mine." Abbie elbowed her friend playfully.

"No worries. I brought you fresh meat." Will jerked a thumb behind him and, didn't it just figure, there was Tye, striding up the path.

Hands *off.* That was the plan. Tye wasn't even going to *think* about kissing Katie Lawson. Or touching her. And definitely not about all the things he wanted to do if he ever got her alone in his camper. She'd been pissed off and embarrassed yesterday. He hadn't handled that whole kissing thing well.

Okay. He hadn't handled it at all.

When Will had given him directions to Katie's place, he'd played it cool. Will knew about yesterday's Segway lesson—the entire jump team knew, thanks to the miracle that was Facebook—but he hadn't said anything. Tye shouldn't have gotten out of the truck. He didn't have to, which meant he didn't have any excuse for being here. He'd cleared hostile-riddled buildings in Fallujah with less unease.

"Tye," Katie said and her voice made an iceberg seem like a tropical destination in comparison to her patent *un*welcome for him.

Her friends stared at him like they were connecting the dots. Or a name with a face. Shit. Whatever she'd shared with them, it didn't bode well for him.

Katie was wearing another one of her seemingly endless supply of sundresses—this one was pink with white polka dots—and a pair of heels. She leaned forward to look at him, or, more likely, give him the death glare, because right now those were clearly one and the same as far as she was concerned, but she also gave him a spectacular view of her cleavage. That probably hadn't been part of her plan, unless she was trying to torture him. The front of her dress pushed the soft curves of her breasts together. Something lacy peeked out over the fabric hugging her chest, so she wasn't entirely naked under there.

No touching, sailor.

He nodded his head to acknowledge her greeting and then Will was making introductions and Tye was filing away intel for future use. Will's wife, Abbie, and Laura Carpenter clearly played for team Katie and learning everything he could was smart. While he did the meet-and-greet, Katie had her fingers wrapped around a plastic flute and was polishing off the contents with the skill of a SEAL hitting a bar for R&R after a particularly tough mission.

"You're forgetting something, Mr. Firefighter." Abbie hopped up off her chair and Will opened his arms. Too bad that wasn't Katie making a run for him, but Abbie had clearly missed her husband. For the entire thirty-six hours the man had been out there in the field.

Will closed his arms around his wife, bent his head and kissed the hell out of her, his hands threading through her hair as he worked his mouth over hers. She stretched up to meet him more than halfway, tugging his shoulders down to her until they were fused together, hip to hip and mouth to mouth.

Laura, Tye couldn't help but notice, watched the pair, a big smile splitting her face. Katie, however, blushed and looked everywhere *but* at Tye. Maybe he still had a chance.

"You guys need to get a room." Laura patted Will gently on the butt. "Somewhere else."

"Got it covered." Will came up for air and grinned. "You ready to go, Mrs. Will?"

"Uh-huh. You betcha." Abbie smiled her goodbyes, then shrieked as Will swung her up into his arms and over his shoulder in a fireman's carry. "If you make me hurl, you're not getting any!"

Will's answer was lost in the playful smack he delivered to her ass as he headed towards their truck. Abbie's goodbye wave to her friends as she bounced away said it all. Tye figured the pair wouldn't come up for air for the rest of the afternoon.

"Those two," Laura said fondly. "You should have seen them at the wedding. It was positively pornographic."

She didn't seem to mind, though, and even Katie was smiling. "They're happy," she said, and for once she and Tye were in agreement. Abbie and Will weren't subtle, but they both seemed happy. Tye's feet, however, seemed glued to the porch. He should be beating a strategic retreat down the path to his truck but he didn't want to go.

Nope. He wanted to pull up a chair and stay. Today. Tomorrow. Hell, the rest of the summer if Katie would have him.

He thought about that for a moment. The idea should have scared the pants off of him. He wasn't a stay put or a commitment kind of guy, other than his marriage to Uncle Sam and Spec Ops. And yet Katie... was an exception to that rule.

Laura eyed him speculatively, then extended a plastic flute to him. He was fairly certain it had been Abbie's. "Drink?"

He shook his head. "I'm driving."

He didn't drink alcohol. He'd seen too many good men try to drown the night demons. Playing bottoms-up with a whiskey glass or a beer bottle was a solid strategy for a few nights, but that plan always went to hell. He'd decided he'd play it safe. No alcohol. No chance of losing control.

"Orange juice?" Laura volunteered at the same time that Katie chimed in with, "Then see you."

Katie's voice had that soft edge that said she wasn't drunk, but that she was just the slightest bit tipsy. Good thing she was home and not driving. He crouched down beside her, ignoring Laura. Citrus wasn't what he needed.

"You and I have unfinished business."

"I think we finished up yesterday," she said darkly. "When you fell off the Segway? Consider that the period to our relationship."

He hadn't been aware that they *had* a relationship. "You asked me to help you work through Kade's bucket list."

"Uh-huh." Her face wasn't encouraging. She shoved her glass at Laura without looking at the other woman. "Fill it up."

He looked at Laura. "Is this your usual Sunday morning plan?"

Katie's hand slapped his knee. "I'm right here."

"Yeah. You sure are."

"What's that supposed to mean?" She eyed him suspiciously.

Laura passed the glass back. Right in front of Tye's face like he wasn't there. "That's the last inch. We've killed the bottle."

He wasn't so sure they had, but Laura was looking out for Katie, and *that* he was on board with.

"Damn." Katie finished the glass, making a face at the orange juice pulp at the bottom. "That's nasty. And, no, I'm not drunk."

His lips twitched. "I never said you were."

"You were thinking it," she accused.

He was close enough that her knees brushed his arms when she leaned over to set her glass on the porch floor. He caught a whiff of her perfume, all those small, feminine tells. Some kind of floral detergent. Warmth of her skin. And Katie... something that was one hundred percent, uniquely Katie. He dimly registered that he was most definitely in her personal space, but backing off was no longer part of the mission plan.

Nor was falling over.

No, the only danger he was in here was of falling *for* her.

"Why are you here?"

"Hear, hear," Laura chimed in.

He shot her a look. "You're not helping."

"Do you want me to?"

Maybe. He ignored her. "We had a deal," he said. "I'll help you with your bucket list project. You'll give me art lessons."

"You spurned my art lessons," Katie pointed out.

Jesus. He shrugged. "I'm free this afternoon. In fact, I'm free right now. We could get started right away. You told me you like to pay your debts. Get square."

"Even-Steven is the best way," Laura chimed in.

The high-pitched, woe-is-me chirp of her Siamese butted into the conversation. Or negotiations. Katie wasn't sure which. Tye flashed her an inquiring look as the chirp got closer. And louder.

She shrugged. "My cat gets lonely."

"And?" The idea of a lonely cat was clearly a foreign concept in Tye's world.

"He brings her presents." Laura laughed, standing up. "He's really partial to socks. You kids be good. I'm going to go check on the Pillsbury special."

Tye waved a hand in Laura's direction, but he didn't take his eyes off Katie's face. She had no idea what was going on in his head, other than this sudden and inexplicable desire on his part for art lessons. She opened her mouth to prod further, but just then Angus waddled through the door, twelve pounds of brown and white angst. Something pink dangled from his mouth.

"Most guys settle for flowers." There was no missing the laughter in Tye's voice.

She squinted at the cat and Angus dropped his present at her feet. *Merde.* That was her laundry day thong. A kind of pink that didn't exist in nature, with little bows marching down the mesh front. She'd left the laundry basket on the bed and Angus had helped himself like he always did. At least it was clean. Probably.

Before she could react, however, Tye scooped the thong up in one big hand and eyed it. "Nice."

CHAPTER EIGHT

Tye had never been a cat person, but he could definitely like Katie's Siamese. Or, more accurately, he could get used to a cat that brought him thongs. *Jesus.* He wanted to do more than imagine Katie wearing that scrap of pink and lace. Maybe she had leather. Or some of those little lace-up bustiers.

Maybe the cat took orders.

Although Tye doubted he'd be that lucky. The cat had the same indignant look on his face as his owner. Order-taking was probably out.

So instead of hot lingerie, he got... art lessons. Definitely not his first choice—or even his second, third, or fourth. Still, he also got to spend time with Katie and that was no hardship, even if he wasn't looking forward to *getting in touch with his inner feelings*—her words, not his—and slopping some representative paint onto a canvas while he discussed said feelings.

Katie grabbed her key to the V.A. center and they headed over to get started. Since Katie was busy pretending Tye hadn't picked up her thong and returned the scrap to her, things were awkward at first. He glanced over to where she was bent over rummaging in the supply closet. She drove him crazy in all the best ways.

She mumbled something half-muffled by the closet—he was almost certain it was her umpteen hundredth *merde* of the day but he was no saint in the cussing department himself—and then she backed out.

"So," she said and slapped a fistful brushes into his hand. "Your weapons of choice, sir."

Her cheeks were still pink, though, so he was fairly certain she hadn't forgotten about the thong. That was okay by him, because *he* had no intention of forgetting either. In fact, he was betting Katie's thong-bearing Siamese would be one of his favorite memories for the next forty or fifty years.

"Whatever you're thinking, stop it," she snapped and thumped a canvas down in front of him.

"You can't read my mind." He dragged the canvas closer. Eight by twelve of pure blank white. He might have managed paint-by-numbers, but this was foreign territory.

"So. Paint." Katie shoved a stack of paint tubes at him.

"This is a DIY project now? No instructions?"

"You've been having nightmares, right?" She waited for his reluctant nod before continuing. "Pick one and paint what you feel. You don't have to remember specific actions or things—just the general impression the dream made on you."

"I don't remember anything about the dreams," he said.

"Uh-huh." Her tone said all too clearly that she didn't believe him. Probably because he was lying his sorry ass off. He didn't *want* to remember, and that was the truth.

"You could model for me. I bet that would help get the creative juices flowing."

She blushed.

"You have." The blush got brighter and he loved that.

Her chin lifted. "Lots of girls do. There's nothing wrong with it and I had bills to pay. *School* bills."

"Girls and guys," he agreed affably. "I'm just having a hard time picturing it. Or maybe not."

Yep. Her blush escalated to about a thousand degrees Kelvin.

"What did Kade think about it?"

She blinked. "Why would it matter?"

He unscrewed a tube of paint. "Some guys don't share well."

"There was no *sharing*," she objected. "I wasn't working in the sex trade. I was modeling."

"Naked."

"Well, he didn't mind." She pointed at his blank canvas. "Start painting."

He stared at the canvas and came up empty. He had no idea where she got her ideas from, but his idea shop was closed. When his brush didn't get to moving, she flopped down next to him, dress strap tumbling down her shoulder. That gave him ideas, but nothing he could paint.

For many reasons.

She ignored his lack of action, rummaging inside her bag for a plastic water bottle. A couple of inches of water sloshed around the bottom. "Damn," she sighed.

"Get me set up." He jabbed his brush toward the empty tabletop. "If you want to paint, give me something to paint."

Not waiting for her answer, he shoved to his feet, dropping the painting supplies on the table. He could fix one problem.

A quick trip down the hall, a handful of quarters, and he handed her a bottle of cold water.

"For me?" She twisted the cap off, hesitated and stared at his empty hands. "We could share."

He dropped back into his chair and fisted the brush. He'd stormed insurgent strongholds and successfully evaded hostiles hot on his ass. He could *do* this painting thing. Randomly grabbing a tube of paint, he uncapped, squeezed, and jabbed his brush into the puddle of goo. Spread the color around some.

Maybe this was the secret to Picasso.

"I need to tell you something," she sighed.

"Yeah?" Damned if it wasn't harder to paint a fucking orange than he'd anticipated. His lines were crooked and—he eyed the sticky blob on his canvas—he was pretty damned certain that the five year-old had painted more realistic fruit. "How does this work?"

"Art therapy?" She patted him on the shoulder. "You use your imagination. Try to paint what you see inside your head. Show me how you're feeling."

He imagined drawing a picture of two people having wild monkey sex on the table. Nope. Probably not what she wanted to see at all. And him? He'd rather be doing anyhow.

"Anything?"

Her hand made a return trip to his shoulder and stayed put. "Pick an ugly memory. Something stressful, something that you've hung onto, but you're ready to get rid of."

"No oranges?" He wasn't a fan of fruit bowls, but he'd take produce over his memories any day.

"Paint Khost," she suggested.

Hell. No.

He looked at her. "That's not something either of us needs to see."

"Are you sure?" She studied him like he was some kind of painting she needed to interpret.

"Why am I the only one who has to paint his deep, dark secrets? I'm only doing this if you do it too."

She rolled her eyes, but she grabbed a canvas and dragged it towards herself. "Is the bad-ass SEAL scared?"

Hell, yeah. He wasn't stupid.

For long minutes, she drew and he watched as her charcoal flew over the white, filling it in with strong, black lines and endless shades of grey. Kade. Of course.

"You're not drawing," she observed, looking up from the canvas. "You really don't have any bad memories? Nothing bothers you at night? Because I'm questioning your ability to stick to the terms of our deal here."

"Bad dreams don't always punch a clock." He stabbed the brush into the puddle of black on his canvas and spread it around some, covering up his orange. "Some memories stick around twenty-four/seven. You miss him."

It was a statement of fact.

"Of course." Her pencil filled in the familiar lines. The drawing wasn't a funny caricature. Looking at it didn't make him want to smile or laugh. Fucking hell, she filled each sweet line with love and emotion and him? He had a smear of paint instead of anything worth sharing.

"I'd bring him back," he said, fiercely. Better than *This is all my fault.* Because Kade should have come home from Khost. Or, at the very least, he should have come home from *that* patrol. But Tye hadn't spotted the danger when that young kid had stepped out of the shadows in the alley. Tye had seen a boy too young to be hiding a gun in the folds of the robe hanging from his thin shoulders. Tye hadn't raised his own weapon. *He hadn't fired.*

Katie looked up at him, her heart in her eyes. "Me too."

So, fuck it. She wanted him to express his feelings about Khost? He could do that. He really, really could. Methodically, he filled the canvas in with thick strokes of black paint.

"I need to tell you something," she said.

"Shoot." *Bad choice of words.*

"Kade and I—"

He didn't want to hear this, he decided. He really, really didn't.

"Yeah?" He knew his voice sounded gruff and like he didn't give a fuck. He should have painted flowers or something moving and soul searching but... he couldn't.

"We weren't really engaged," she said in a rush. "It started out as one of his jokes and kind of snowballed."

His brush shot over the edge of his canvas and painted the table. Nice going. "Are you kidding me?"

"Nope." She set the charcoal down and turned toward him, her knees brushing his thighs. When had she gotten so close? "Kade only asked me to marry him as a joke."

"Marriage isn't a joke." He knew that much. Marriage was forever and promises.

"No," she said and he hoped to God that wasn't sadness he heard in her voice. "It wasn't a funny, ha-ha kind of thing. He just wanted to protect me. Make sure no one hit on me in the bar. And then it... snowballed. It was our secret and we were friends and it was just something we did." She stopped and thought for a moment. "That sounds stupid, when I say it out loud like that. Doesn't it?"

"I don't know," he said. What it seemed like was exactly the kind of trouble Kade got into. It was also one of those bittersweet moments, followed by a side of relief. He only wished Kade's death was another joke and his buddy would pop up at any moment, yelling *surprise*.

"You're mad," she said and fidgeted with her paintbrush. And the canvases, the tubes of paint, and her hair. That gave her a brand-new streak of blue to go with the brown, but now wasn't the moment to tell her.

"I don't know," he repeated, because that was the truth. "I don't know how I feel, but how about we paint some more and I'll figure it out?"

Tye painted with single-minded intensity. Katie checked the clock on the wall—discreetly, of course—and was surprised only half an hour had passed since she'd dropped her bombshell. Somehow, *not* telling Tye had seemed wrong. She wasn't sure what they had between them, but it was definitely more than a bucket list. So she really needed him to clue her in about his feelings.

If, of course, the guy a) possessed any and b) was capable of articulating them. Which was doubtful, given his reaction to painting a picture about said feelings. He didn't know where to start. Which was about as far from great as one could get.

"How about now?" she said, because she had to have some kind of an answer or sign from him. He focused with single-minded intent on the canvas in front of him. Which was neatly lined with alternating rows of black and gray. Great. If those colors were any indication of how he felt, she'd screwed it up badly.

"Khost? Or me?"

He raised a brow. "Excuse me?"

"Your painting," she said. "Why gray and black? What experience are you thinking about?"

He shot her a look she couldn't interpret. Well, she got the frustration part of his glare. There was something else there, too, though, that she couldn't quite make sense of.

"I'm not mad at you, Katie."

"That's a relief," she said lightly.

He sighed and set down the canvas. "You really weren't engaged?"

"We were, but then he broke it off. He said he wanted me to get out there for real."

He picked up her canvas and examined Kade's face. "He's always here."

No. Kade wasn't. And *that* was the problem.

"Not literally," he said, "but in your head. In mine. We're sitting here together because you want to remember him."

"Everyone keeps telling me to move on," she protested. "But there's nothing wrong with remembering him."

He thought for a moment. "Remembering's good. Nobody wants to forget Kade. We just don't want you to stop living your own life, Katie. You have to do stuff for *you* and not because it's on some damned stupid list Kade probably put together when he was twelve."

That kind of attitude just pissed her off. "You make me sound like some kind of martyr. We didn't even have a real relationship. We were all kinds of made up."

He shook his head. "I don't know whether the two of you would have made it to the altar or not, but what you had was real. Just kind of—" he paused for a second, that smile she loved tugging at the corner of his gorgeous mouth—"mislabeled. Kade cared about you. Hell, I saw that every time he got one of those goddamned letters from you."

"That doesn't sound like caring." She set her brush down. Tears blurred her eyes and, darn it, she was so sick of crying. She'd cried oceans. How could she not be all dried up by now?

"We were all jealous," Tye said bluntly. "He'd read us parts, show us some of your drawings, but every man in the unit wanted those letters for himself. We wanted to read the whole thing, to have you waiting for us back home, ready for us to come back."

His words warmed her up where she'd been cold. "I don't think I could handle an entire unit."

"Yeah." His head dipped closer, his lips brushing her cheek. "Angel, you're still stuck on that ménage to do item and that's just one bonus guy."

If she turned her head, she'd be kissing him. Or close enough. He'd pushed her away the other day, on the Segway. Or, she thought, the relationship light bulb clicking on in her head, he'd pushed *himself* away.

"I don't want to talk about Kade." She meant it too.

His head rested against hers. "That's a start," he agreed. "What *do* you want, angel?"

"Tye—"

She turned her head and, yep, they were definitely close enough to kiss. Her lips brushed his. There. No mistaking that for anything but what it was. A quick, sweet kiss, lips brushing on lips in a quick reconnoiter.

She pulled back, just in case she'd totally misread the situation.

Again.

Point made. She looked up at him from beneath her lashes. "I want kisses."

He ran a hand over his chin. "Yeah. That wouldn't have been on Kade's bucket list."

"Kissing you?" She grinned. "His loss."

"What kind of kisses?" he growled. "Tell me what *you* want, Katie."

"You," she said. "I think I want you."

"Be sure," he warned, but he was already moving, lifting her and depositing her on the table before she could so much as squeak, and darn it—she shouldn't have found his effortless manhandling so sexy. But she did. God help her, but she did. And then he leaned into her and she was so, so lost.

"Tell me something," she started, but he cut her off gently.

"I like your dresses," he said. "That's one thing."

He placed his strong hands on her thighs and pushed slowly. His fingers were nowhere close enough to her naughty zone, but a warm, solid presence. Tempting. She *might* have wriggled a little. Not that she was admitting to anything.

"You've got paint in your hair," he said. "That's two."

Well. *Merde.* She twisted, trying to find the offending spot.

"That's not a bad thing," he said roughly. "Paint's a good look for you and this is supposed to be my art therapy, yeah?"

It was broad daylight, she was on the table at the veteran's center, and she was loving it. Loving *him*. Tye Callahan was a lethal weapon.

"Just kisses." His mouth moved over her temple, deliciously rough. "And maybe some touching. That's all we're going to do for right now."

"Are you promising me a later?" she challenged. Knowing where she stood was good.

"Absolutely." He removed one hand from her body—she fought back a whimper of protest—and reached for something beside her. And that *something* stroked over her collarbone, a soft, erotic tickle that had her coming up off the table.

"Tye—" He had one of the paintbrushes fisted in his hand, was wielding it with wicked concentration. A clean one, the last rational part of her brain recognized, before she gave up thinking and jumped feet-first into the pleasure.

"Shhh," he whispered. "We're painting, right?"

"Sounds like a plan," she agreed. Painting had never been so decadent. Or sexy.

He drew the brush down her arm, swirling a small circle on her palm. *Oh, yeah.* His other hand slid beneath her, cupping her ass and anchoring her. He teased her, drawing naughty patterns that made her groan and shiver. Her lashes drifted shut and the pleasure was even more intense. Her and Tye. The brush and the sweet, erotic dark.

"I'm going to do the other one," he whispered roughly, switching his attentions to her other arm. *So good.* She wiggled and arched into his touch, the brush teasing new nerve endings to life.

This was *Tye*. He tugged, pulling her bodice down to her waist. He cursed and she bit back a small smile. Because, yeah, she'd worn her very best underwear today. Thank God. The little half-corset that just fit beneath the top of the dress was a lacy pink and white, the soft cups pushing her breasts up into two perfect mounds that even she liked looking at, feeling all kinds of sexy even if the corset had been her secret. Tye obviously liked the corset too.

"Damn, angel," he said roughly.

"Uh-huh," she agreed happily, opening her eyes. His eyes were hard and hot, focused entirely on her. Four slow flicks of her fingers later, the corset parted and Tye's breathing got a whole lot rougher. He traced her breasts with the brush, smoothing the bristles over the curves with an erotic tickle and then circling her nipples. Little whimpers escaped her because, damn, he *was* good.

He slipped his hand out from beneath her ass and slowly pushed her skirts up. That was promising, but she had no idea what to do with her hands. Or maybe that was the haze of pleasure, because she wasn't thinking clearly. But the feelings were all there, sweet and hot and building.

"Hang on to me," he suggested and her hands shot right to his shoulders. *Perfect.*

"Tye—"

"This art therapy is working for me," he said roughly.

The brush moved over her thighs. *Oh... yeah.*

"And I really, really like your panties."

The brush stroked her center. Up. Then down.

Oh.

Again. Please.

And he did. Soft strokes followed by a deeper touch. *Harder.* His fingers teased the edge of her panties before slipping beneath to find her. He touched her and the pleasure shimmered through her, followed by the inescapable blush painting her cheeks because this was one of those all or nothing moments and she was all out there. Exposed. What if he didn't like what he saw? Or she didn't do this right? And yet it felt so good. *He* felt so good.

"Beautiful," he muttered roughly. "You're so goddamned beautiful, Katie."

And, strangely enough, those blunt words relaxed her, had her closing her eyes and losing herself in Tye. His knuckles nudged aside her panties and his warm breath teased her there, where he'd touched. *Looking*, but okay. He liked what he saw. His breath caught, followed by more kisses. Life might not have a happily-ever-after in store for them, but plenty of happy-for-right-now.

And much, much later as she sighed and tightened, he lifted his head for just one moment and asked, "You absolutely sure this is what you want, angel?"

"Yes," she said, more moan than word. "Yes, please."

And please he did, pushing her gently over the edge, holding her tight to him as she came.

CHAPTER NINE

Katie had paint up and down her back. She knew that because she'd discovered Tye's grey-and-black canvas jabbing her in the back when she'd come back down to earth. *Merde*, but her SEAL could kiss.

Everywhere.

She blinked up at the ceiling and tried to catch her breath. Okay, she definitely didn't need to pursue the ménage option, because one guy was more than enough for her. *Tye* was more than enough. She summoned enough energy in her post-orgasmic bliss to lift her head and look at him.

Head pressed against her belly—his lashes tickling the soft curve she still wished would miraculously disappear, he cradled her hips with his hands. She couldn't tell if he was meditating, drinking her in, or catching a nap, but he seemed content, like a large cat, even though she was almost certain she was the only one who'd finished. Charcoal streaked his T-shirt where she'd clutched him and the paint in his hair said she must have landed an elbow in his canvas when he'd got really, really wicked with his brush.

The table top, however, was no Sealy Posturepedic. She shifted, but the new spot was just as hard as the first. Tye lifted his head and looked at her. Well, he'd *looked* at her before. At other parts of her. Parts that definitely hadn't seen the light of day in more months than she cared to remember. Parts that weren't for public consumption, except—she fought back the urge to giggle—when apparently they *were*.

"Hey," he said. "You still with me?"

Lying sprawled out on the table should have been awkward. It was definitely messy. But it felt right.

Wicked, too.

That was a new feeling for her and she liked it. Liked it—liked *him*— a lot.

"The table's hard," she offered, when she really wanted to say *Holy moly, you're amazing* and *Can we do that again? But on a mattress this time?*

Wordlessly, he scooped her up in his arms and settled back in his chair, legs stretched out in front of him as he cradled her close.

"Better?"

She was voting *yes*. She looked around the room, but it was still the same place it had always been. She, however, definitely looked worse for wear. He'd started out painting the canvas, but then he'd painted her. She had hand-shaped marks on her breasts and, she twisted—yep—on her ass.

She pointed to a particularly egregious smear of paint. "Was that necessary?"

"I owed you. The day we met?" His arms tightened. "That pink paint didn't come out of my BDUs."

"Consider us even."

There was a moment of silence, then he said, "I'm pretty sure I feel better. You could make a fortune with this art therapy stuff."

She snorted. "I'm pretty sure you did all the heavy lifting. Plus, they can arrest you in California for charging money for that."

"For *that*?" He laughed. "*That* has a name, Katie."

He loved the way she blushed. Not five minutes ago, she'd been whimpering and hollering his name, but *now* she was embarrassed. He probably shouldn't tease her. Hell, he *knew* he shouldn't.

He grinned. But that wasn't going to stop him.

"Next time," he said, "I'm going to make you say *it*."

She squirmed, trying to work her way to the edge of his lap, but he held on. He wasn't done with this holding business.

"Fantastic." She slapped a hand on his chest and pushed. "That's what I'm calling *it*. Okay?"

"Works for me. I can also do stupendous, fabulous, and mind-blowing."

She shook her head. "I'm a lucky woman."

"You bet." He set her on her feet and stood up. "We've probably pushed our luck just about as far as we can here."

She didn't say anything, just buttoned and tugged and then started shoveling her things back into her bag. He thought about pointing out that dumping a wet paint canvas into her bag was going to make one hell of a mess, but her mind was clearly elsewhere. So he helped her where he could, held the door, and trailed behind her out to the sidewalk. Yeah. He didn't do *follow* well.

There was a moment of awkward silence on the sidewalk. He didn't know what she wanted or expected. She didn't look at him as she fished in her bag for her keys—and came up with red fingers. Yeah. A mess all around.

He knew what he wanted though.

More kissing. More Katie.

So... into the breach he went. "Ride with me? Back to my place?"

He told himself he wasn't holding his breath. They'd had a *thing* back there in the V.A. center and just because he'd thought it was hotter than hell didn't mean she wasn't entertaining a regret or two. Or two thousand. Damned if he knew what she was thinking. But his heart kicked into overdrive when she opened her mouth.

She smiled. Thank God. She smiled. He'd done something right. "I can take my car."

"But I'd like to drive you."

"But—" She hesitated.

He wanted to drive. Because, yeah, then she couldn't slip out on him. Couldn't leave him without at least a little please and thank you, but that wasn't the biggest reason. He liked the idea of her trusting him, both to make the sex good and to make her feel safe. She hesitated and he thought *say yes*.

"I'm driving my car. I'll be right behind you," she said and he took what he could.

He dropped a kiss on her mouth, right there on the sidewalk where everyone could see. She stiffened briefly before melting into him. She tasted sweet. Sweet and hot, a taste he wouldn't be forgetting. Ever. Just kissing could be enough, but she'd promised him more.

"Drive safely," he said, pulling back.

"I'll see you in ten," she agreed.

He put her into her car, then swung up into his truck, put it in gear, and pulled out. If he drove fast, he could be home in ten.

"It's not much," he warned, hand on the camper's door. In fact, his temporary-for-the-summer digs were about as standard as they came. She nodded and he pushed the door open—no one bothered with keys out here—and stood back so she could go in.

"No kidding." She widened her eyes comically as she slid past him. The camper was standard hitch-up-and-go fare. He had a double bed, a built-in table, and two chairs. The place also offered a tiny, can't-swing-a-cat-in-it bathroom but that wasn't the kind of floor space he did his entertaining in. Still, he wished he could offer her more. Something his, not borrowed. But he couldn't. Not today. He shoved the regrets into the do-not-open box, stepped in, and closed the door behind him. The snick as he flipped the latch announced his intentions loud and clear.

She stood by the table, fiddling with the straps of her purse and, yeah, the moment ranked way up there on the awkward scale. This was just sex, he reminded himself. Sex with Katie Lawson, true, but he'd done this before. *Man up.* He never hung back. He *engaged.*

Her bag thumped onto his table and she eyed the door.

New strategy.

"We should get the paint off you."

The jump team had a set of solar-heated showers, but that was too public and the camper's built-in shower was about ten square feet of white plastic that combined the toilet with the shower plumbing. There was nothing romantic about showering with your ass planted on the toilet and there was no room for two, either.

Snagging a washcloth from the cupboard by the shower, he ran warm water over the cotton.

"Come here, angel."

"Tye—" She fidgeted and he could practically read the thoughts crossing her pretty face. Doubts. Unease. And something else he couldn't identify, but he'd bet had everything to do with the fact that he wasn't Kade and she wasn't the kind of woman who had casual hook-ups.

He turned off the tap. "You having second thoughts?"

"And third and fourth," she admitted.

"Come here," he repeated. "Let me see what I can do about that. The door's still going to be right there, no matter what you decide."

She bit her lip. "You wouldn't mind if I decided not to stay?"

"Angel, I'd mind a whole damned lot, but that's not my call. If you don't want to stay, you go. This is about what *you* want."

"And you." She took a step toward him. The RV was so damned small that the move put her with touching distance. He stretched out a hand, tugging gently on her wrist gently. She let him pull her close.

"The two of us," he agreed.

He ran the warm cloth up her arm and followed with his mouth. Her pulse pounded against her skin, like a scared thing wanting to come out. "Good?"

"Mmm-hmmmm. Do the other," she demanded.

He laughed, warmed up the cloth, and repeated the long, slow glide up her skin. Turning her in his arms, he found the zipper running down the back of her dress. One long, slow pull and the dress fell away, caught on her arms by the straps. She looked over her shoulder at him and, thank God, that was *hunger* on her face as he undid her corset.

"You've definitely got paint here," he said roughly, running his hands over her back, pressing his thumbs into the sensitive muscles by her spine.

She arched into his touch, her pony tail spilling down her back. "You mind?"

"Not a bit." He kissed her some more, trailing his mouth up the straight arrow of her spine, licking and tasting.

"Better be sure," she moaned. "Because I'm pretty sure I've got paint in all sorts of places."

"Lift," he ordered gently. He braceleted her left wrist with his fingers, pulling her back so he could ease the strap down her arm. Then repeated the process with the right until her dress slipped down to her hips. One hard tug and the fabric pooled around her ankles and her fuck-me shoes.

"Have I told you how much I love your shoes?" His voice came out as a hoarse growl, but she just laughed, wriggling back towards him as she stepped out of her dress. That left her in just her panties and that corset bra thingy she'd tormented him with at the V.A. center. He let his fingers do the walking, undoing the little hooks that marched between her breasts and down. Yeah. Right where he wanted to go.

Her hands closed over his when he reached for the lacy ribbons holding her panties closed over her hips. Their fingers tangled and together they slid the scrap down. Naked. He had Katie Lawson completely, gloriously naked.

"You have too many clothes on." Her protest was half-sigh, half-pout.

"I can fix that." He hesitated. "You can say *no*, Katie. Any time."

He didn't want her pressured into anything. He wasn't quite sure where her head was at with Kade, but even if their engagement had been a game and the game was over, she'd still loved his friend. In all sorts of different ways. He hadn't asked because it really wasn't any of his business, but he'd have bet the camper that Kade and Katie were friends with benefits. So maybe she wasn't quite ready to hop into bed with him.

Or maybe she was. A guy could hope.

She grinned at him and his heart turned over. "What I want," she said, "is to say *yes*. Over and over. Think you can handle that?"

Thank you, Jesus.

He could feel the answering grin tugging at his own mouth. "Hooyah. I'm your man."

"Glad we got that settled."

She hopped onto his bed and *that* got his blood pressure rising, along with other parts of him.

"My turn to watch," she announced, parking her ass on his pillows and drawing her knees up to her chest.

"Always," he said. Bending over, he unlaced his steel-toes and set them to one side. Then he pulled the T-shirt over his head and popped the button on his jeans. His fingers stilled. *Jesus.* She was watching him alright. When she looked at him... Slowly, he shucked the jeans down his thighs and stepped out, reaching down to swipe his clothes from the ground and lay them over the chair. Then he headed straight for her.

First impressions counted and, wow, Tye made a hell of a strong impression. If the man packed a punch without his shirt—and their run the other day was definitely one of her new favorite memories—he was even more spectacular. All he wore were the dog tags around his neck and his chest was smooth, sun-tanned skin everywhere she looked. He'd also clearly put in the work it took to get six-pack abs and arms of steel.

He was roped and muscled, pure power in a sensual Tye-sized package.

She dropped her gaze because she wanted to see *everything*. His erection was as impressive as the rest of him. Tye prowled towards her—there was no other word for it. He moved smoothly, fluidly, with a predatory look in his eyes like he just couldn't *wait* to eat her up.

Which was fine by her.

More than fine really, because her girly bits were still doing the happy, happy dance from his attentions at the V.A. center. Suddenly in a hurry, she scooted beneath the blanket and sheet. Late afternoon sun filtered into the RV, turning the place all shades of cozy, the built-in furniture painted golden-yellow in the light. The sheets smelled like Tide and the outdoors, plus something both indescribably masculine and Tye.

"You've got incoming," he growled, dropping a knee on the bed. The mattress squeaked and gave beneath his weight.

"Oooh. Sexy talk." She scooted over, making room for him. It was his bed after all.

He snaked an arm around her waist, dropped and rolled. She ended up sprawled on top and, who would have thought? They almost fit on his bed. Mostly. Enough. Her legs hugged his hips as she braced her hands on his shoulders.

So good. She pressed closer, wanting him everywhere at once and he obliged,

his hands moving over her, rough-gentle as he kissed her. Not enough, she decided, leaning down into his kiss. Their tongues stroked, tangled. She could have kissed him for hours and yet she also wanted to get to the really good parts.

The really, really good parts.

She slid her hand down those washboard abs of his, drinking in the sudden tension in his body. Wrapping her palm around him, she fisted him. Slick and hard, he strained against her fingers. She rubbed the tip where he was silky smooth, then dragged her palm down again.

His fingers were on the move as well, parting her where she was slick and wet for him in a sweet invasion. She tightened her legs around his hips, her heels digging in as they touched and teased.

He rolled her beneath him, breaking away briefly to yank open the bedside table drawer.

"Condom," he managed.

Not necessary. "I'm on the Nuvaring."

He hesitated. "You sure? I've always been careful but—"

Her little burst of happiness had nothing to do with the sex, not really. "We're good." She cupped his ass with her hands, urging him forward.

His dark eyes watched her, assessing. He didn't move, but the tip of him teased her entrance. "If you're sure."

"I am." And then some, she thought, right before he slid deep and sure inside her, banishing rational thought. She pushed up and he met her, more than halfway. They were on the same wavelength, just this once. She had no idea if this happy state of agreement would last, or if they'd get out of bed—because, at some point, that had to happen—and then they'd go back to fighting for control of their relationship but right now... right now, they were perfect.

Together.

Then she lost her train of thought again, got lost in the in and out, the delicious friction of Tye moving in her and on her.

"You're a shrieker," he said long minutes later and the satisfaction filling his voice had her slapping at his shoulders.

"Shut up. Move more," she groaned—or possibly yelled—and then, sure enough, he did something that felt impossibly good and she was yelling his name as he took them both over the edge.

Tye was fairly certain they'd rocked the camper.

Literally.

He collapsed on the bed, rolling onto his back and pulling Katie against his chest. She grunted, but came sliding over his skin. Boneless, he decided, knowing he probably had a big, sappy grin stretching his face. He slanted a glance down at Katie. Her eyes were closed, but she wore a matching grin. Mission accomplished.

Outside, someone slapped the side of the camper and hollered a cheerful admonishment. Tye was fairly certain the words included *lucky* and *dog*. That was the truth, and the guys outside didn't even know who he had in here.

"Were we that loud?" Katie didn't move.

He considered lying to her, but she'd figure it out the minute she left the camper and half the jump team was staring at her. "Yeah. You were."

"All your fault," she mumbled and the grin on his face got wider.

"You could probably knock that ménage off your list now," he whispered into her ear. "I think that was a volunteer."

She opened her eyes and grinned at him. "I've got my hands pretty full."

"Maybe you'd like to try again," he suggested. "In French this time. Just so we can check something off the bucket list."

"*Oui*," she said and that was all he needed to hear.

CHAPTER TEN

The next few weeks, Tye came and went, heading out on his smoke jumping missions or training missions. The practice wasn't the problem; it was the real deal that had her chewing her fingernails to the quick. When the plane took off on those days, Tye's jump and the lightning storms were the icing on the cake. She knew from listening to Kade that what seemed like a simple, no-bad-news strike could actually be the start of a killer fire. A few sparks smoldered in an old tree and then—poof—seemingly out of nowhere, dry wood exploded into fire.

On high alert, the spotters in the national parks watched for those first betraying twists of smoke on the horizon. Catch the baby fire soon enough and a hotshot team might have time, if they got in there fast, to knock down the fire before it grew out of control. If it was too late, if the fire was too remote or too out of control, Tye's team went. The boys in the plane got there faster.

She levered up on an elbow and stared at Tye, lying on his stomach, face buried in his arm. He'd slipped into her room late last night. She'd given him a key after a thumbs-up from Laura. After two days out in the field, he still smelled faintly of smoke with a hint of pine and fresh air, although his hair was damp from a recent shower. If he were anything like Kade, he'd sleep for a month of Sundays.

Don't think about Kade. Not here. She ran a hand lightly down Tye's back, savoring the hard press of muscles, the heat of him beneath the cotton T-shirt. Kade had been her friend with benefits and a fiancé of convenience. If what she'd felt for him hadn't been a passion worthy of romance novel territory, the feelings had still been something special. She could have happily spent the rest of her life with him if he hadn't decided it was time for them both to move on and find something more.

Her *something more* snored softly in her bed.

Tye Callahan.

Tye was hers temporarily, no more permanent or real, relationship-wise, than Kade had been. She was fairly certain they were friends too. She liked him.

Too much.

He wasn't a keeper and he wouldn't be sticking around in Strong much past the end of fire season. She knew how the jump team worked. The Donovan brothers might have taken up permanent residence in Strong at the end of last summer, but that had been part miracle, part accident. Those bad boys of summer had fallen in love, met their match in three strong women, and the rest was history. They'd chosen to *make* their firefighting lifestyle work.

Tye hadn't. Heck, she wasn't even sure he realized that there *was* a choice waiting to be made. He'd be like the rest of the guys on the Donovan team, moving on when the summer wrapped up and the fires died down. The other jumpers would fan out, working various part-time gigs or enjoying the downtime, while Tye would... well, she didn't know what he'd do, but her money was on re-upping. Will had mentioned to Abbie—who had oh-so-conveniently let it drop, a concerned look in her eyes—that Jack Donovan had offered to hire Tye on permanently. And Tye had turned the job down.

So that was that. He had no intention of sticking. He shifted in the bed, dragging the pillow over his head. He was also definitely hunkered down for the next couple of hours. Since there was no getting back to sleep now, she got out of bed and padded across the floor to her desk by the window. Sketches of shoes covered the surface. Yay for shoes and having a secret, guilty passion that didn't involve the man on the bed.

Tye swam up through layers of sleep. His muscles protested as he stretched, because forty-eight hours in the field had done a number on him. His eyes felt gritty, a sure sign his body wanted more sleep. *Hell.* He tightened his fingers on the pillow he'd apparently decided to use as a sunshield. Cracked an eye and got a full on view of white cotton with girl eyelet trim. Yeah. He wasn't in his bed.

He was in Katie's.

He patted a hand around the bed, but, nope, she was unaccounted for. The sheets on her side were empty—and cool. She'd been up for some time. What kind of a boyfriend did that make him? And wait, when had this become dating? They had a shared interest (thank you bucket list). And they had sex (an even better shared interest from his point of view). It wasn't anything more than that. Couldn't be. Sure, he'd thought about staying put in Strong. He didn't have to re-up with Uncle Sam. He'd done three tours of duty after and, as a Navy SEAL, he made a difference. Or, he *had*.

He'd let his team down. He hadn't had Kade's back that night in Khost and, as a result, Kade hadn't gotten to come home. Kade was dead, the kind of screw-up Tye couldn't fix. Ever.

He knocked the pillow back and… bingo.

Katie perched on a stool by her desk, working intently on something. She muttered under her breath as she tilted the form and, he grinned, those curse words sure didn't sound like French to him. He'd tease her about that later.

She'd piled her hair up on top of her head in one of those gravity- and logic-defying messy up-dos women liked. He liked it too. Her soft curls were pretty, but the style also exposed the curve of her neck as she bent over her desk. Huh. She was working on a shoe.

She'd told him she made shoes, but he hadn't grasped exactly what that meant. The smell of leather and glue floated his way, almost as familiar as the look of intense concentration on her face as she stacked small circles of wood together. She got that same little crinkle between her eyes right before she came. He didn't know the first thing about shoes—and, really, if he was honest, he didn't know *anything*—but the pair she was working on were beautiful.

Abso-fucking-lutely beautiful.

She was soft. Not in a bad way, it was just that—life hadn't given her hard edges, hadn't forced her to suit up in emotional armor. He touched her and she gave. Jesus. He was clearly no fucking poet, but he knew one thing. He liked Katie Lawson.

Far too much.

He also liked—*loved*—having sex with her.

He sat up in the bed, silently shoving the sheet back. Lost in her own world, she didn't notice the movement behind her. Plus, Uncle Sam had taught him a thing or two about stealth movements. He went in fast and silent. Waited until she set the baby shoe down—he wasn't stupid enough to mess up her work—and then slid onto the stool behind her, wrapping his arms around her.

He leaned in to examine the shoe. "You're good."

The hard, male presence behind her was a surprise, but a good one. Lost in her work, she hadn't seen him coming, but he felt right. She leaned back into him, tipping her head up so she could see his face.

"I know."

The words sounded complacent but it was... true. She made beautiful shoes.

"What do you do with them?" He sounded genuinely curious.

"Nothing." She shrugged. "Sometimes, I wear them."

When she looked at the shoe taking shape on her desk, her heart squeezed. The shoe was gorgeous, a sunshine-yellow pump with black laces and a kitten heel that made her want to smile just looking at all that happy color. Never mind that she had no place to wear it, no one to share it with. Laura shared Tye's obsession with practical footwear, but Abbie was always good for a raid on the Macy's shoe department. Katie had made the most delicious pair of ballet flats to go with Abbie's wedding dress, slippers that looked like flower petals—white daisies with diamante centers and a small blue ribbon on the heel for *something blue*—wrapping around her friend's arches.

"Nothing?" Tye plucked the shoe out of her fingers.

"Hey—" She reached, but he held the shoe just out of her reach. "Don't mess up my heel."

"I wouldn't dream of it," he said solemnly. "So you're not planning on doing *anything* with this shoe?"

She twisted on the stool, trying to see his face. "No. Of course not. It's just for fun."

"There's no *of course* about it. A shoe like this deserves a future." He grinned down at her.

"It's just a shoe." It killed her a little bit to say that, but it was the truth. The shoe was a shoe, made for standing on, for tramping here and there. Or, she eyed the delicate heel critically, for waltzing around a ballroom, conquering a boardroom, or resting its deceptively strong and very graceful self on a manly heart somewhere. Or not. Because who was she kidding? None of those things had ever happened to her, regardless of what she had on her feet.

Tye set the shoe back on her desk and wrapped his arms around her.

"I hate to disagree," he said softly and she bit back a snort. Tye *loved* disagreeing. Especially with her. "That's not just a shoe. It's—"

"What?" she prompted. How far would he take this? "Are you volunteering to be my fit model and try it on?"

"As if. That's a damned pretty shoe. It's art."

"Shoes aren't art."

"Why not?" He nuzzled the side of her neck.

"Have you ever seen a shoe in an art gallery?" Tye's kisses made logical arguments difficult, she thought muzzily.

His lips left her skin—darn it—and he nodded at her shoe. "Have you tried? Evan's fiancée runs that gallery here in town. You should ask her."

God. She was in trouble here. This *thing* she felt was so much more than attraction or even liking. Nope. Tye might be big and gruff on the outside, but he was marshmallow sweet on the inside. He said the nicest things without even realizing it, because that was just the way he was made. She had a problem. He fixed it. Things were simple in Tye's world.

She was the one who made them complicated.

She had a bucket list to knock off, so the hot sex was simply an added bonus. Unfortunately, while her head was on board with that sentiment, her heart was making plans of its own.

"Katie?" Tye prompted when she didn't answer. "You should try it. Do something for you."

Yep. Her heart was headed straight into the danger zone.

"I—" She didn't know what to say.

"Just show her the shoes," he suggested. "Let her know you'd be open to exhibiting."

"Let me show you what I'd be open to," she said throatily and pointed towards the bed.

Katie had no idea how she'd ended up standing on the sidewalk in front of Faye Duncan's art gallery, clutching a banker's box of shoes. She needed her head examined. Or an escape hatch.

Merde.

She pushed open the door and stepped inside. The gallery was a welcome cool spot, the air conditioning refreshing after the warmth outside. Natural light flooded the wide, open space, and Faye clearly liked her firefighters. Photographs of the firehouse and the jump team were everywhere Katie looked, entire walls of gorgeous, hard-bodied men. Faye had selected fun scenes, like the guys hosing down the fire trucks, but added darker pictures too. In one shot, the guys were headed back from the field, faces ash-streaked and grim.

"They lost that one." Faye came up behind her. "The fire gobbled up fifteen-thousand acres and thirty homes. It came down out of the hills and devoured a housing development."

Faye Duncan was in her middle twenties and radiated happiness and laughter. Being around her was almost enough to counteract the butterflies in Katie's stomach. Of average height, with an expensive-but-growing-out shoulder-length haircut, she wore a filmy pink skirt and a white tank. She also needed a shoe intervention, because she sported a pair of dusty white rubber flip-flops.

Poor shoe choices aside, Faye was a talented photographer. The firehouse shots were easy money to shoot, but the fire scene? She had a hard time imagining the sprite-like woman standing out there surrounded by smoke and flames. And yet that was clearly what Faye had done, gone out into the thick of the disaster to capture the images.

She and Faye were acquaintances. They'd done the potluck and Sunday brunch thing, plus the other woman was a frequent visitor at the fire camp because her fiancé had grown up here in Strong. None of that made pitching a new exhibit any easier. Her shoes couldn't compete with the firefighters in the smoking hot department.

"They're beautiful," she said. Faint praise, but she didn't know what to say. Faye had captured the jump team perfectly. Serious, playful, determined.

Faye grinned and a big-ass diamond ring winked on her left hand as she gestured towards the photos. "In more ways than one. God was kind to Strong. I'd love to shoot your guy."

"Kade would—"

"Not Kade." Faye's face softened. "Tye. Your new guy, right?"

Right. She hesitated, not sure what to say.

"Shoot." Faye made a face. "Did I put my foot in it? I just assumed you guys were together."

"Why?" she asked, curious. What had Faye seen?

"You just look—" Faye smiled. "Like you belong together. The way he touches you, looks at you. There's a connection there. Plus, he's gorgeous and Kade wouldn't want you to sit on the dating sidelines for the rest of your life. So why would you look and not touch?"

"Yes," she said and it sounded good. So she said it again. "Yes, he's mine. But I don't think I can loan him to you for a photo shoot."

Just the thought of Tye stripping down and facing Faye's lens had her heating up—and wanting to smile at the same time. Tye was intensely private. Starring front and center in a gallery exhibit would be hell for him.

"Bummer." Faye bumped her shoulder gently. "Work on him for me, okay?"

She sucked up her admittedly low supply of courage. "I had a question for you."

"Shoot." Faye grinned at her. "I'm all ears."

This was crazy.

Crazy stupid, crazy good, somewhere in between... she didn't know which.

"I design shoes and I was wondering if you'd consider exhibiting some of my work." The words came out too fast and she ran out of breath at the end, but the words were out.

Faye's eyes dipped to the box Katie clutched. "Did you bring show-and-tell? Fantastic," she added when Katie nodded.

Faye led her over to a cluster of low sofas in the center of the gallery. She sat down, waving toward the spot across from her. "Wow me."

So Katie did. Or tried. That had to count for something, right? She pulled shoe after show from her box, unwrapping her treasures and talking Faye through what she loved about each one. After five minutes, she forgot to be nervous. After ten, she forgot to shut up.

Fifteen minutes later, Faye held a hand up to stem the tide of words and turned a sassy red leather pump over in her hand. "I would kill to wear these. I was supposed to get a loaner exhibit of gold miner drawings from San Francisco. They cancelled." She shrugged. "If you want the slot, it's yours. I can't promise that you'll get rich or that there will even be media coverage this late in the game."

"You're saying *yes*?" *Don't pass out on Faye's couch.*

"Absolutely." Faye looked lustfully at the shoe in her hand. "You bet. Although, if you decide to sell these babies, I want first dibs on this pair."

They discussed the logistics and Faye promised to draw up a contract and drop it by the bungalow later tomorrow.

"You should make custom shoes," Faye suggested, walking Katie to the door. She still hadn't let go of the red pump. "*Bespoke*. That's the word, right?"

"I'd never thought about it." She fished the pump's mate out of the box and handed it over. Faye beamed. "I wouldn't have thought there was a huge shoe market in Strong."

Faye shrugged. "We get all sorts of day-trippers stopping at the antiques store and you could add a web storefront, maybe focus on custom bridal shoes. You should think about it. Plus, I saw what you did for Abbie. I want that for me, but different."

Wow. She'd never considered going into business. Stepping outside, she eyed Strong's main street speculatively. Maybe she should do a little real estate and lease shopping? Just in case Faye had a point?

CHAPTER ELEVEN

Katie had had her hands full getting her shoes ready to exhibit. She might be last minute filler for Faye's gallery, but that didn't mean Katie wasn't giving it her best shot. Faye had given her an opening date of two weeks after their initial meeting. She'd spent her days picking shoes to exhibit, discussing lighting, presentation and press with Faye. Whenever Tye came home, she was on the phone, on the computer or bent over her damned desk working.

He'd wanted this for her. He just hadn't realized it would mean temporarily giving her up. He'd taken to spending the night in his camper and she hadn't said anything. He wasn't entirely certain she'd noticed he was gone.

Tonight was the big night, however. He pulled his truck up in front of her bungalow and got out, but she was already coming out to meet him, clearly eager to get the show on the road. Her black cocktail dress had a front that just skimmed the tops of her breasts and tempted him to run a finger over those tempting curves. The dress hugged her tightly, stopping way too soon above her knees. And her shoes... Those were definite fuck-me shoes. Purple satin pumps with a four-inch stiletto heel and a ribbon tie that curled wickedly around her ankles and tied in a saucy bow at the back. He had no idea how she navigated the sidewalk and climbed up into his truck, flashing him a glimpse of her sun-tanned thighs and... *Jesus. Christ.* Yeah. He liked her thong, too. In fact, he was damned certain the black-and-white zebra print scrap would drive him crazy before the night was over.

He cleared his throat.

He wasn't sure the peekaboo show was an accident, either.

He shut the passenger-side door, went around and climbed in. Looked over at her because some things had to be said.

"You look gorgeous," he said gruffly.

His usual dress code was BDUs and combat boots. Fancy dress parties were out of his league. Even he knew he couldn't wear denim to Katie's gallery opening. It would have been disrespectful to everything she'd accomplished. He'd put on the only other thing he had. His dress uniform.

"You too." She beamed at him. "I love a man in uniform. And thanks for picking me up."

Her happy smile was contagious. He could feel the corners of his own mouth curling up as he tipped his head in acknowledgment. "Thought I wouldn't make you walk in those shoes."

Minutes later, he pulled up at the gallery. Light spilled out onto the sidewalk, drowning out the stars overhead and the black expanse of sky. The entire jump team appeared to be assembled on the other side of the plate glass windows (because he might have called in a few I-owe-ya's just as insurance that Katie's opening would be packed). And the shoes... yeah, Katie's shoes were the star of the show. Faye had perched one sexy number after another on top of tall white pedestals, letting the shoes speak for themselves. Glamorous. Sensual. Playful. Tye had plenty of adjectives to describe what he saw, but he still had no idea how Katie did it.

When they went in, Faye immediately carried Katie off, to introduce her to various media people. While Katie mingled, the Donovans closed in.

"You've met Faye?" Jack handed him a crystal flute of champagne.

"Uh-huh." Tye tried to figure out how to juggle the delicate glass without wearing his drink on his dress whites. "She seems real nice."

Rio swooped in beside him, deftly trading the flute for a beer bottle. *Thank. God.* "She's reeling you in."

Tye eyed Faye. She seemed harmless enough. Plus, she was engaged to Evan Donovan, as the enormous rock on her ring finger advertised. "Why?"

Rio draped an arm around Tye's shoulders. "You have heard of the calendar, right?"

He searched his memory. "The charity thing?"

"That's the one." Rio steered him towards the back of the gallery. "Faye wants to do another one and you're fresh meat, my man. If you're not careful, you're going to star front and center. Evan has to let Faye have her way with him—he signed up for it when he popped the question—but the rest of us are free to run."

Rio stopped them in front of a small side gallery. And... Jesus. Tye fought the urge to back pedal. To ring out and cry uncle. Twelve by twelve black and white shots of smoke jumpers lined the walls. Apparently, naked was a prerequisite. He'd also had no desire to know what Evan Donovan looked like fresh out of bed.

"Wow," he got out, borrowing Katie's word.

"It's something, isn't it?" Rio moved away and took a swig of champagne from Tye's flute.

"Don't scare him off." Jack strolled towards them. "There are worse things than getting naked for a good cause."

Not in a million years. There was no way Faye would convince him to strip down and pose.

"You'll get used to it," Jack said. "It's kind of a prerequisite of working the jump team long-term. Unofficially, of course, because I'm trying to avoid sexual harassment lawsuits."

Rio just grinned.

Settling down, staying put in Strong hadn't formed any part of his plans when he'd pulled into town two months earlier, and his summer was almost over. He looked over at Katie. She was smiling, waving her champagne flute to emphasize some point. Tye loved the look of pure happiness on her face. She, on the other hand, clearly loved this.

Jack slanted him a look. "Job offer's still good."

He could stay. He could make a home with Katie, make sure that smile stayed on her face each and every day. He tested the thought. He'd read her letters to Kade, had anticipated each new drawing. She loved laughing, loved living. And she did both so well. He knew he was broken inside, that he had a dark inside he had no business bringing near her.

"Maybe," he said. "I might do that."

When the gallery opening wrapped up, Tye took her home. Her home, but she was pretty certain he felt comfortable with her even if he'd been strangely AWOL these last two weeks. When he opened the truck door, she was reaching down to untie her heels. The purple satin was one of her prettiest efforts, but her feet hurt. Quick as lightning, he pulled her out and into his arms, her shoes dangling from his fingertips.

"Sweep a girl off her feet, why don't you?"

He gave that quick, hard bark of laughter she loved. "Only you, honey."

A quick key insert at her front door and then he headed straight down the hall to her bedroom. She leaned her head back against his shoulder, happy to enjoy the ride for a moment.

"Good night?" He asked the question gruffly, looking down at her as he strode toward the bed.

"You bet." Tonight had been the best.

And she wasn't ready to be done. She was keyed up, excited by the adrenaline rush of seeing her shoes—*her shoes*—perched on all those sexy little pedestals and doing media interviews for a handful of California papers.

Do something for yourself, he'd said.

He was right.

"Tye?"

"*Oui?*" He pulled back the covers and set her down on the bed, before turning away and undressing like they'd been married twenty years. For a moment, she watched him, enjoying the show. He took off his jacket and unbuttoned his dress shirt, leaving everything neat and folded and as dramatically unlike her own exploding closet as possible.

She *definitely* wasn't ready to be done for the night. She rose up on her knees. "I'm going to do something for myself now, okay?"

"Whatever you want, angel." He came over, his hands reaching for her hips to steady her.

She felt behind her for her zipper. Yoga was good for many things, including getting her own zipper. The black cocktail dress fell down around her arms. One good shimmy and she knelt before him in just her thong and thigh-high stockings.

He inhaled sharply. "How is this working out for you?"

She reached for his waistband. "I promise I'm going to enjoy myself a lot."

When she leaned forward, baring him for her touch, her mouth, he got a whole lot louder. *Oui.* Definitely this counted as doing something for herself, because hearing him gasp her name, his rough pleas for more, for *her*? She could happily do this all night.

CHAPTER TWELVE

It was fucking pitch black.

So dark Tye couldn't tell if his eyes were open or shut. He lifted his hand in front of his face and, nope, he couldn't see that, either. A quick pat of his side revealed his weapon wasn't where it belonged, which meant he was defenseless. He had to be ready to shoot. Delay and people died.

He inhaled, sharp and fast, the dark closing in around him. *Breathe.* Night vision would come. It always did. He counted to ten, sucking air like a diver under too long.

On ten, he forced himself to listen. Was the Humvee on fire? Had he driven too fast, bit it at last? He couldn't hear the other man who shared the cab with him. Kade. His wingman. The first thing he'd learned was that worse was always outside, worse was coming for his team and he couldn't do a goddamned thing about it. Hatred roamed the streets outside the Humvee, armed with guns and sticks and a homemade napalm that burned so fast and hot that no foam could put it out.

Nothing.

No guns thundering. No wounded men moaning through clenched teeth, because some shit hurt so much that the sound tore free no matter how hard or how much you wanted to hold it in. Hell, not even the tick-tick-tick of the motor cooling down because he'd killed the engine. Was he pinned down?

Something—*someone*—moved behind him, clothing rustling. The gentle whoosh of breathing assaulted his senses. He wasn't alone.

Rolling swiftly, he pressed the intruder into the mattress.

Mattress. Not the Humvee with its vinyl seats and hardware, but Serta goodness. Firm, with sheets that smelled like Tide and dryer sheets—and a floral perfume that teased his memory.

He had a female pinned on her side. Her breathing no longer soft and even. Startled gasps, each in and out pushing her breasts against his arm. He registered silky material dislodged by his roll and pin. A warm, plump breast resting on his arm. That was better than his usual meet and greet in the dark.

Keep it together. He wasn't pinned down. Wasn't trapped in the Humvee as a mob of angry Afghans moved in. That was the nightmare. This was the reality. Wasn't it? Or had his head reversed fact with fantasy?

He curled his hand around the breast and rolled the nipple between his fingers. A SEAL didn't know who was friend or foe. The woman offering tea today could be gunning for him tomorrow. His nine-to-five included roadside bombs and hidden snipers. A street wasn't simply a street and no one—absolutely no one—could be trusted.

"Tye?" A sleepy voice floated out of the dark towards him, and his panic faded some. He'd told her to sleep facing away from him because he jerked in his sleep and tended to come awake fighting, reaching for his gun or the knife. She knew better than to get too close.

"Yeah." That was who he was. *Tye*. Not *sailor* or *Officer* or *infidel*.

"You can't sleep?" She didn't move, didn't demand he let her go. She knew better. Just like she knew what was coming now.

"No talking."

"Okay," she breathed. He gave her nipple a careful pinch, savoring her sharp gasp.

Her nightdress had that kind of crisscross bodice, all pretty lace and silky material. Thin straps crossed her shoulders and held the front up. He hooked his fingers in the straps and tugged. His knife would have done the job—beneath the pillow, his head reminded him—but she didn't like knives. She'd made that clear.

Instead, he pushed the material down. Khost? Or somewhere else? Jesus, he didn't know where he was. *Wrong*, his head told him, but his heart pounded hard and he anchored himself on her. With her.

"You're the one pinned down," he growled.

"Yes," she whispered back and reached back for him. He stilled, legs wrapped around hers. He was naked. No camo, no survival gear. His heart pounded so loudly, he couldn't hear her breathing, his chest tightening painfully. Vulnerable. *No*. She was the one at his mercy.

She tried to shift, but he controlled her body effortlessly.

"Stay put," he growled in her ear. Wrapping her hands in one of his, he used his thigh to open hers while he pushed her nightdress up to her waist. His hand moved over her stomach, savoring the rounded curve and tracing her belly button until she squirmed.

"Please." Was the rough word a plea for permission or a statement of intent? Hell if he knew. He rubbed his erection against the small of her back and she pressed into his touch, welcoming him. *Yes.* She'd said *yes.* This was okay, this simple, raw connection between that kept him sane in the darkness. He ran a hand down the straight line of her spine.

"Tye," she groaned.

That was his name. He held onto the word like a lifeline, knowing he was all kinds of fucked up. He couldn't give her niceties or pretty words. All he had was what was left of himself and how could that be enough?

"Katie," he rasped, remembering where he was. Almost. He wasn't in Khost. Wasn't on patrol. *Jesus. Christ.* The relief almost made him boneless, but he teased her, sliding his dick along the cleft of her ass while his fingers stroked through her folds.

"I'm right here," she whispered and she was and he was wrapped around her so tight. He knew this woman. Knew this bed and this place. He should sit up and swing his legs over the side of the mattress. He should get his boots on the ground and his ass out the door because he didn't belong here.

Instead, he carefully pushed his fingers into her hot, slick depths, because that was the one place he did belong now. While he fought his lungs for control, sucking air in and out, his chest heaving, he drew his fingers up and down, enjoying the slippery, silky feel of her. She was impossibly soft. And wet. He could smell her and this was what home smelled like. Tide and Katie.

He didn't belong back here in this world of parks and supermarkets and shopping centers. He couldn't jog down a goddamned path without checking for explosives, half-expecting every footfall to be his last. He breathed rough on the trail and not because he was out of shape. Nope. It was because he was scared shitless and running, running, running. Not that he'd admit that. He nodded his head and barked *Sir* and *Ma'am* at the oncoming tide of joggers and ran faster.

Katie arched her back, small, happy noises escaping her.

He could do *this*.

He touched her, tunneling his fingers deep inside her while he buried his face against her neck and breathed. Her hair tickled his nose and cheeks. He found a secret, hidden spot inside her and crooked his finger, rubbing. With the little scream he remembered and loved, she tightened around his fingers, the muscles in her thighs and ass clenching and quivering.

"Moving," he rasped out the standard SEAL move call.

"Now," she demanded and he notched himself against her opening and pushed. He banged into her and she met each thrust with a backward thrust of her hips, chanting his name in a desperate, glorious litany. The bed creaked, the headboard slamming into the wall. She stilled, coming with a long, slow gasp he recognized.

Katie.

He poured himself into her, marking her. Now she'd smell like him and her. *Them.*

"Wow. That's an awesome way to wake up." She didn't *sound* upset. She rolled over, wrapping her arms around him.

He ran his fingers over her mouth, tracing the smile there. He was in Katie's bed, Katie's arms. Not Khost. He didn't ever have to go back there.

"Did I hurt you?" he asked roughly.

Jesus. Christ. What kind of man was he?

"No." She sounded certain, but he ran his hands over her, looking for hidden damage.

"Tye." She rubbed her hand over his arm. "Tell me what's wrong?"

Part question, part concerned demand, he didn't know whether he appreciated her words or wanted to beg her to shut the hell up and leave him alone. He was working through this. He *was*. If there'd been a way to ring the bell and quit the nightmares, he would have taken it. He really thought he would have.

He wasn't a quitter.

He wasn't.

"Nightmare. You don't want to know," he said, stalling for time.

She moved closer and, *Jesus*, she was almost naked and the word was a prayer.

"You need to tell someone." She wrapped her hand around the back of his neck and rubbed. "Maybe you can tell me."

"Why?" he asked and he really wanted to say *why do you care?* Of course, the answer was probably because Katie was nice, the kind of person who took a grizzled vet out for coffee and watched out for a feisty five-year-old in her art class because the kid's mom was too frazzled to think straight and needed the hour to herself. She let people skip paying because otherwise they might not come, forced to choose between an hour of fun and paying the light bill, the insurance bill, or any one of a dozen other bills.

So, no, her asking didn't mean anything more than that. She was nice. He was hurting. Sure, they'd had fantastic sex and he was pretty certain they were friends. Good friends. Friends with benefits. It was nothing more than that, although even that was so much more than he deserved.

"You worry me," she said.

That was the last thing he wanted to do.

"There was a kid on the street." He was starting the story in the middle, but she'd catch up. Or not. She'd asked and now he was telling, the words coming fast and hard. "We were on patrol, Kade and I. We hit an IED with the Humvee and got out. We were okay, which was a miracle, but there were insurgents laying down heavy fire and it was time to get out of there. A kid came out of the shadows. He was smiling at us and I figured he was just curious."

There was no label he could put on that moment the kid fished in the folds of his oversized robe. A wide grin had split his face, making him look like a child playing dress-up, except that then the kid had produced an AK-47 from all that fabric instead of a toy and had pointed it at Tye. And that's when he'd frozen because, fuck... that kid couldn't have been twelve. More like ten, even though the kid's eyes had been going on eighty.

"He had a gun."

"Oh, Tye," she said. Maybe she didn't know what to say either, because her hand rubbed faster.

"I should have shot him right then," he said fiercely. "I should have raised my weapon. And. I. Didn't. Kade had to finish the job for me and that's what got him killed, because he followed that kid and there was an IED and..."

"Boom," she said softly.

Yeah. Some things didn't need more words than that. Boom, and it had all been over in one terrific flash of heat and light. Nothing left but him, the Humvee, and a big-ass crater he couldn't possibly fill.

"*Merde*," he whispered against her hair. "That about covers it."

No. It didn't cover *it*. She had no idea what the right words were. She pulled Tye closer and wrapped her arms around him, hanging on tight. Not that strangling him would make him feel better, but he was so alone. So sure that Kade's death was his fault.

"Bad shit happens," she said when they were cheek-to-cheek. "In both French and English."

"Yeah," he agreed, voice hoarse. "I'm with you there."

She ran her hands down his back, rubbing. Pulling him close. Her big tough guy had a soft side. He worried. He believed he'd fucked up big time. She didn't know if he had. She hadn't been there, didn't know what had really happened on that street in Khost.

And it didn't matter. She knew who he was now. Kade wouldn't have wanted his friend to beat himself up over what was either not his fault or was an understandable mistake. Shooting a kid, even if he'd been armed, wasn't the kind of man she'd fallen in love with. She hurt for him, wanted to fix what was broken, but some things he had to do for himself.

The man she'd fallen in love with.

She knew how that had happened, but the *when* eluded her. Instead of worrying, however, she wrapped her arms around him, pulling him tight.

"You're a good man," she said. "And you have to let it go. Get on with your life."

She'd undoubtedly have to get on with her own.

Because, however she felt, this was a temporary, summertime romance.

He didn't say anything, but some of the tension eased from his shoulders. Long minutes later, she felt the moment he relaxed completely, losing himself in sleep again.

Right now, right this moment, Tye Callahan was hers.

CHAPTER THIRTEEN

The cell phone on the nightstand buzzed and played a raucous refrain of Big & Rich's "Save a Horse, Ride a Cowboy." Kade had programmed his favorite song and personal barhopping anthem into Tye's phone on one particularly unforgettable night off in Khost. Tye opened his eyes, fishing for the phone automatically with his left hand, while his right hand wrapped around Katie. Sprawled on his chest, she made a little snorting noise.

The ring tone pealed out again.

Which was impossible, now that he was awake to do any kind of clear thinking.

Bringing the phone up, he squinted at the number he'd never expected to see again. *Kade's* number dialing him.

"Tye" Katie's sleepy voice was half-muffled as she mumbled into his chest. "Is everything okay? Is Jack calling you in?"

They didn't jump at night. Ever. That was a basic safety regulation. If their asses were on the ground, it was fine to work through the night, but the planes didn't go up after dark. State of California cut the pilots off at dusk. It was—Tye eyed the phone—three a.m.

"Did you turn off Kade's cell service?"

She shook her head, burrowing her face deeper Tye's chest. "I didn't. Can't speak for his parents though." She yawned. "Why?"

"Kade's number is calling me."

She sat bolt upright. He'd imagined this moment a hundred times after that last night in Khost. Kade, calling to say that it had all been some kind of horrific mistake and he was coming home. He'd hoped that would happen. Katie, however, had *believed* it would. What if she'd been right?

No. It was impossible.

What was more likely was that someone had got their hands on Kade's phone.

"Answer it." Katie groped for the phone and he sat up.

Damn it. He didn't want to answer, didn't want to dash the hope blossoming on her face. She was probably imagining a dozen different homecoming scenarios right now. Thinking about Kade and what he meant to her.

Tye wanted her thinking about *him* like that.

Double damn.

Kade couldn't possibly be on the other end of the line. Kade was dead.

He punched the talk button on the button. "Yeah?"

And... the miracle happened.

"It's Kade," said a familiar voice on the other end. The voice was faint and tired-sounding, half-drowned out by background noise.

Tye didn't know what to say.

"Jesus Christ," he eventually blurted out, not sure if the words were a curse or a prayer.

"Not quite." Kade sounded tired. "But apparently I'm back from the dead."

Katie froze. Tye threaded a hand through her hair, rubbing the back of her head. How must she feel?

"What? How?" He didn't know where to start. He wanted to know the details but relief overwhelmed him. He hadn't gotten his best friend killed. He looked down at Katie, staring up at him. Hell. But he'd slept with his friend's girl.

"It's a long story." Kade clearly didn't want to share the details over the phone.

"Where are you? Are you okay?"

"I'm on a plane. I'll be landing in San Francisco in four hours, then I'm heading up to Strong."

Katie's nails dug into his chest and Tye was almost certain she hadn't taken a breath since he'd answered the phone. He wanted to reassure her, wanted to hand the phone to her but... yeah. This went beyond awkward.

"Where are you at?"

And there it was. The question Tye had been dreading.

"I'm in Strong," he said.

The silence stretched out long enough that Tye wondered if the connection had dropped.

"You asked me to look out for Katie if something happened," he said. Katie shoved away from his chest and, yeah, she was breathing now. A deep, pissed-off, sharp exhalation.

"Right. Thanks. If you're there—" Kade hesitated.

"Give me your flight number and I'll pick you up at the airport."

"Thanks." Kade rattled off his deets and then there was another pause. "No one else," he said. "I don't want a welcoming party."

Hell. Tye wanted to ask what kind of injuries Kade had sustained, because Tye had heard that tone from dozens of other veterans calling home to say that they'd be coming home. Most of them. Minus a few pieces others might or might not notice the loss of.

"Welcome home," Tye said and he meant it.

Even if he did feel like the damn cuckoo in the nest.

"I knew it." Katie whispered the words. Then she shrieked them. Kade was coming home, and if that wasn't cause to bounce around the room like a Mexican jumping bean, she didn't know what was.

"Katie." Tye said her name and there was a note in his voice that almost brought her back down to earth. Almost. Instead, she yelled Kade's name again because, darn it, she'd been right. Kade was on his way home.

Someone banged on the door. Her roommate. "I'm opening the door," Laura bellowed in a voice that had to carry out onto the street. "But I'm not looking. Just tell me no one's dead."

Tye tossed her his T-shirt. "You might want to cover up," he said dryly.

Right. She looked down at her very naked self. Some things, a roommate didn't want to see. Tugging the shirt over her head, she flung the door open.

Grabbing Laura's hands, she swung her roomie around in a crazy happy dance. Laura went along with the dance move, craning her head to look over Katie's shoulder at Tye. "Whatever you're doing to her, you should stop."

He shrugged. "This isn't my fault."

Laura squinted at him. "You're sure?"

"Kade's landing at SFO in four hours."

"Wow." Laura looked at Katie for confirmation. "I did not see that one coming."

She hadn't either. She really, really hadn't. "It's true. He just called."

"Pinch me," Laura ordered. "This could be a dream."

Tye tossed her the cell phone. "No need for violence. Kade just called. Check the number."

"Wow," Laura repeated, catching the phone one-handed. She checked the screen and chucked the phone onto the bed. "You were right, Kats. One hundred and ten percent right. You're going to have to give back that flag his CO gave you."

"Kade's not dead. Kade's coming home."

Laura sank down on the edge of the bed, "Holy—wow. That's great. Overwhelming and completely unbelievable, but great. Are you going to greet him? Is he coming here?"

Katie wasn't sure whether Laura meant Strong or their house, but the answer had to be *yes* and *yes*. She turned to Tye.

"I'll ride with you to the airport." She'd cancel the afternoon's art lesson. It wasn't like Mr. Rickerson would really notice.

"I'm going alone." Tye shook his head and glared at Laura. "I'm standing up now, so you've been warned."

Laura grinned. "Don't let me stop you. If my roomie's bringing home hot firefighters, I'm entitled to sneak a peek."

But she averted her eyes as Tye swiped his sweatpants from the chair and pulled them on. The casual movement had his thighs flexing in a way that demanded attention. And his spectacular ass... was all red scratch marks where she'd held on good. Heat flooded her face. She was surprised Laura hadn't banged on the door sooner, because she was fairly certain she'd been loud.

Tye. Kade. Oh, God. She was sleeping with Tye, but Kade was on his way home.

And yep... Laura had come to the same conclusion. She made a face.

"Kade's my..." What was he?

"He said no welcoming committee." Tye grabbed a clean T-shirt from his duffel and pulled it over his head in one swift move.

"I'm one person." She would have liked to throw the fiancé business in Tye's face, but the savage look in his eyes said that wouldn't fly right now. "He'll want to see me. Even if we're not—" She waved a hand, because, really, there just weren't words to describe her relationship with Kade.

"He's been gone for months," Tye said. He reached for his boots. "Obviously, he had a reason for not coming home. Since Uncle Sam declared him dead, I'm betting he was taken prisoner. And, after the explosion I witnessed, I doubt he was uninjured."

"You would know." And... cue the bitter tone in her voice. Jesus. That wasn't like her.

Tye gave her a long look. "Yes. I would. So whatever's happened to him, whatever state he's in, he's not ready to face the world yet."

She folded her arms over her chest and inched towards the door. Tye was going to have to go through her to get to his truck. Or out the window. Based on the look on his face, he was considering that option. "He called you."

"Yeah." Tye's cautious agreement didn't give an inch.

She was fairly certain the window exit had just rocketed up his options list. "Not me." She wouldn't let that hurt.

Kade hadn't called her. He'd called Tye first. Or instead—because she still hadn't heard her own phone ring.

Laura stood up. "I'll be out in the living room if you need me." She beat a hasty retreat.

"Why would he do that?" she asked.

He eyed her calmly. "Ask him that. He's the only one who has that answer, Katie. Maybe he had my number handy. Maybe he figured it would be easiest to reach out to another SEAL. I'm going," he said. "I'll pick him up, bring him back here. Then you can sort out whatever needs sorting."

"Running away?" she mocked.

"Don't." He swiped his duffel bag from the chair, the motions all neat and precise like him. He didn't like messes or loose ends, which was too damned bad for him, because tonight she was both.

"He wants you, not me," she said. "This has always been about him."

Dark eyes watched her carefully. "Do you really want to go there?"

"I want the truth." She was tired of his questions.

She'd known from the start that their relationship was only temporary, but her mistake had been in believing they could have an actual relationship. Instead, she was a box to tick on Tye's to do list. Rather like her borrowed bucket list. This had never been about *them*—it had been about Kade.

Tye rubbed a hand over his head. "Kade *asked* me to look out for you, all right? And I was happy to agree. All of us in the unit talked. We all knew that there was a good chance a mission would head south and we wouldn't make it home. Kade had you waiting for him and he wanted to make sure you'd be okay. Hell, you were all about Kade with that list of yours. I'm not the bad guy here. You wanted help. I gave it. I'm going."

"Leave," she mocked as he headed out. The door shut quietly behind him—Tye wasn't the kind of guy who slammed things to make his point—and moments later she heard the muted roar of his truck engine.

CHAPTER FOURTEEN

Kade was waiting at the curb when Tye reached San Francisco International after breaking at least half a dozen different traffic laws.

Shit. Tye hadn't managed to get there in time for the pickup either.

He pulled the truck into the passenger loading zone and swung down, grateful for the airport security guards barking orders to *move on* and shrilling their whistles. By the time he'd tossed Kade's duffel bag in the back of the truck, his friend was already parked in the passenger-side seat.

After they pulled out, however, the words still didn't come. The San Francisco freeway was no place for a heart-to-heart, even if Tye had been qualified to lead one. Start one. Hell, whatever it was people did when they had emotions to share and dirty laundry to air.

"You hungry? Thirsty?" Yeah. Like that wasn't lame.

Kade shook his head, fingers tapping on the armrest. "I'm good."

There was an opening. "You sure?"

Tye took his eyes off the road long enough to eyeball Kade. The man sported no visible injuries, but he was fully dressed and Tye had seen enough men, soldiers and sailors, to know that the scars weren't always on the outside.

"My leg's busted up some." Kade admitted. "A couple of broken ribs, bruises. We've done more damage on training missions."

Tye doubted it, but calling Kade a liar wouldn't help either.

Instead, he focused on getting back to Strong as fast as he could without causing a wreck or getting pulled over. He didn't know if Strong could fix what was wrong, but it was where Kade had been headed, so Tye would get him there.

"How's Katie?" Kade didn't take his eyes off the highway.

"She's good," Tye said gruffly.

"You see much of her?"

Answering that sounded like about as much fun as doing jumping jacks in a minefield.

"You asked me to look her up," he stalled. "She was pretty busted up when she thought you were dead. We all were."

Kade cursed. "It's one hell of a mess, isn't it?"

"You're home," Tye pointed out, guiding the truck into the lane headed for the Bay Bridge. "Things are looking up."

"Maybe." Kade was silent for a bit, staring out the window at the lights flashing by. "She's stubborn. She wouldn't give up on you. They handed her a flag and a stack of medals, and she still insisted you were coming back."

"Yeah." A note of pride filled Kade's voice. "She's something special."

"A hell of a woman," Tye agreed.

"Right." Kade looked over. "So..."

"So Katie said the two of you were over. That you were never really..."

"Engaged?"

"That."

"I asked. She said *yes*. Were we planning on walking down the aisle? I don't think so. Why?"

Uh. Yeah. That was the question. "Katie and I spent some time together," he said carefully.

Kade nodded. "She's great."

"Yeah. But if the two of you are—"

Kade tilted his head back again the seat. "Damn. I don't think I'm ever straightening this leg out again."

Decoy.

That was okay. Tye reached for the radio, fiddled the dial until he found a country singer lamenting pissing his life away. Perfect.

The music filled the hours, as did a stop for gas, but eventually Strong appeared in front of his windshield and there was no putting off the moment. Kade was home. Tye parked the truck.

"I'll get the duffel. Katie will want—"

"To see me." A weary grin split Kade's face, but he got out of the truck faster than he'd gotten in.

Tye followed, more slowly and not just because he was on luggage duty, then stopped halfway up the walkway.

Yeah. He *so* had no business being here.

Katie must have been waiting by the window, because she was already out the front door, flinging her arms around Kade and dancing him around the porch. Laughing. Crying.

Laura took the duffel bag from him. He hadn't seen her coming. "Tough break."

"You have no idea."

Katie tugged Kade inside. Nope. Because he hadn't had known either.

How he would *feel*. What it would *mean* to see Katie tugging Kade inside the house, leaving him outside.

Katie might have dragged Kade into the house, threading her fingers through his. Maybe. Possibly. She wanted to squeeze hard and then harder, to make sure he was really there. *Kade was home.* She was fairly certain she hadn't said one coherent word since Tye had driven up and Kade had gotten out of the truck.

Tye.

Tye hadn't come in. She didn't know what to make of that. Later. She'd figure it out later.

Kade stumbled slightly, slapping a hand against the wall to steady himself. "Slow up."

"Are you okay?"

"Why does everyone keep asking that?"

"Because you were declared dead three months ago. *IED* and *crater* were mentioned. I assume whatever kept you off the grid had to be pretty intense." She spun around. "It wasn't a secret mission, was it?"

Kade sighed. "Nope."

This close, there was no missing the lines of pain and exhaustion carved into his face. He started moving again, though, and she went with him like she always had. If he'd flown in, he probably hadn't gotten much sleep.

"Hey," she said, opening her door. "You can talk to me. Or there's a bed right there with space in it for you."

"Thanks." Kade limped over to the bed and flopped onto it, facedown. "I'll be human later, I promise."

"There's no rush." She ran a hand down his back, but he didn't flinch. Just settled deeper into her bed, his face half-buried in the pillows. Moments later, the steady up and down of his back told her he was asleep. She couldn't begin to imagine what he'd lived through.

But he'd lived.

He was *home*.

Everything else could be worked out.

Moving to the bottom of the bed, she carefully untied his boots and eased them off his feet. Climbed back up beside him and watched him sleep.

Home.

CHAPTER FIFTEEN

Laura eyed the box addressed to Tye sitting on Katie's bed. "You have to use the U.S. post office? You're not seeing the man anytime soon?"

Katie really didn't think so. "We're—" she wondered how she could possibly explain her non-relationship to Laura. She hadn't seen Tye in the week since Kade had come home. He'd avoided her like she'd come down with the plague. Or acquired a fiancé.

She looked down. So she'd bought him a pair of shoes. A thank you present for his part in bringing Kade back to her. Or... well, okay, it might have been a *hey, remember me?* She'd added a little doodle of his closet with three pairs of shoes in it. She had no idea what he'd make of the gift.

"Taking some time apart, exploring options, screwing up the hottest sex of your life?" Laura offered the list of options, no smile on her face.

"That about sums it up." She sat back on the bed. She'd made a mess of the packing tape. Good thing Tye never went anywhere without that knife of his, because she'd apparently gone for overkill and used half a roll on the box.

"Uh-huh." Laura sat down on the bed and wrapped an arm around Katie's shoulders.

She wanted to hold it together. She really, really did. Somehow, though, there were tears dripping down her face and the box was polka-dotted with wet spots except for the three hundred or so places where the tape reflected back the water.

"He was just helping out a friend," she sniffed.

Laura made a noise somewhere between a snort and a laugh. "You don't have sex to help a friend out. Not a guy friend, at least," she added judiciously. "We girls can get way more into taking one for the team."

"He came here to Strong because that's what Kade planned on doing." Unfortunately, that wasn't really the part that bothered her.

"Misguided sense of loyalty. Definitely a guy." Laura sighed. "I'm not sure how any of them survive to old age."

"Then he looked me up because he told Kade he would. If something happened."

"That's not a bad thing," Laura pointed out, "although full disclosure should have happened shortly after he met you and not when Kade came back from the dead."

"That's what I thought."

Tye was a good guy and he'd meant well. He'd come here with a plan to honor Kade's memory. She knew that, even if she really hated his execution. After all, she'd wanted to work through Kade's bucket list herself. She completely understood not being able to let go and needing to *do* something. But she hadn't passed Kade's list off as her own. She'd been honest about what she wanted.

Which was Tye.

Damn and double damn.

Laura swore. "You fell in love with him. You broke the cardinal rule of hot summer sex and got attached."

Katie stared down at the box. Too bad she couldn't wrap up all of her feelings that neatly. Or maybe not so neatly. Cat hair stuck in the packing tape and there wasn't a straight line in any of her handiwork. She had no idea how she could make shoes but taping up a box eluded her. It was probably one more reason why the post office had moved to self-stick boxes.

"Maybe," she admitted. "Probably."

"Love is like pregnancy. You can't be maybe, possibly or half pregnant—or in love." She frowned. "You're not pregnant, are you?"

"God. No."

"Good. Then I'll take this to the post office for you."

"You're living the good life out here." Kade dropped into Tye's lawn chair and cursed as he stretched his leg out in front of him. In the week since he'd come back to Strong, things hadn't changed much in the leg department. "Maybe they should have cut the damn thing off."

They both looked at his leg and then at the cane in Kade's hand. Tye would bet Kade hated relying on a stick.

"Two is definitely better than one," Tye said.

"True." There was a moment of silence, then Kade closed his eyes, letting his head thunk back against the camper. "Still hurts like a bitch though. You got a beer for an old friend?"

And that was it. Eight words that answered all of Tye's questions. Questions like: Do you blame me for that last night in Khost? And: Are we okay?

"Yeah." He got up and grabbed a beer from the cooler inside the camper. Popping the top would have been overkill, so he settled for handing the cold can over.

"Thanks." Kade settled back further into his chair.

Tye opened his own can and took a sip. The beer probably didn't contain enough alcohol for this particular conversation. "What happened?"

"You saw the kid." Kade sounded certain and he was right, damn it.

"I saw him. I—" The words burned in his throat. "I did nothing. The kid started to fire, you stepped in, and then both of you were just..."

"Gone," Kade supplied. "IED. If you hadn't been standing on the other side of the Humvee, you'd have been toast. The blast did a number on my leg, knocked me to the ground."

Tye waited. Kade hadn't been lying on the ground when the rest of their unit had swept in for a rescue op.

"Insurgents dragged me off. I spent the next six months enjoying a luxurious spa vacation in a basement in Khost."

Tye had a pretty good idea that those six months had been beyond hellish. Kade's tone said *don't ask*, however, and he could fill in the blanks for himself. He didn't need the details until and unless Kade felt the need to share.

"Rough?" he asked, hoping his friend understood Tye was good for whatever was needed. He wasn't going to push, but he'd do whatever it took to get Kade back on his feet. He wasn't sure *fine* and *one hundred percent* were in the game plan anytime soon, however.

"It wasn't easy," Kade admitted. "Eventually, I worked the bars over the window free and wiggled out, found a U.S. patrol and they patched me up. It's all good."

Tye doubted that. He admired the fierce determination in Kade's voice, but some things were harder to shake off than others. Six months of insurgent torture and off-the-radar captivity weren't easy to take.

"If you say so." *Jesus.* He should say something else. Something that let Kade know Tye had his back now and wouldn't let him down again. Instead, all he had were platitudes. "You need something, you tell me. I'm on it."

"Appreciate it." Kade worked on his beer like it was a lifeline.

"They do a decent patch job on you? The leg okay?"

He'd seen how Kade levered himself down into the lawn chair. That leg wasn't one hundred percent any more than Kade's head was and what Kade had shared in the truck didn't begin to cover it.

"I'll make it work," Kade said fiercely. "I'm going to be jumping. I'll be back on the line."

Tye knew his friend would, too. Kade was one determined son-of-a-bitch. "No re-upping?"

Kade shook his head. "I'm done. Three tours were enough."

He hadn't seen that coming any more than he had the IED and the kid with the gun. Kade ringing out, Kade quitting the SEALs... he'd never even considered those possibilities. Downtime, yes, because a body could only take so much. But a permanent hiatus? Not in this lifetime.

Like he'd read Tye's mind, Kade said, "Don't."

Tye stalled for time, taking a swig of his own beer. "Don't what?"

"Don't beat yourself up over that night. You saw a kid."

"That kid wanted to shoot your ass with an AK-47."

"Yeah." Kade sighed. "And I shot him right back."

"You did the right thing. You did your job." He hadn't.

"Did I?" Kade opened his eyes and looked over. Tye could read the pain and discomfort in those dark eyes easily, even though he was no fucking genius. New lines fanned away from the corners. Too much time squinting into the desert sun and holding on when every nerve in the body screamed *stop*. Not enough time laughing. "I wonder about that every fucking night, Tye. You saw a twelve year-old boy. I saw a target. Which one of us is the better person?"

"It wasn't about being the better person." Hell. This was the last thing he wanted to talk about. "It was about being the better SEAL."

"Maybe. I have no idea." Kade set his beer can into the cupholder Walmart's genius engineers had built into the chair arm. "I can't go back until I figure that out though. How about you? Are you re-upping?"

"I was planning on it." What had happened to his simple *yes*? When had going back become a hypothetical, something he was *planning* on—but hadn't committed to yet?

"What about Katie?" Kade asked, going straight to the heart of the problem.

How did you ask the guy you got mostly killed if you could have his girl? And, to be fair, it wasn't like Katie was something they could pass around anyhow. She was a person. An amazing, loving, hot-as-hell woman he just might want to stick around for.

"Shit," he groaned and rubbed his hand over his face.

"That sums it up," Kade agreed.

"She wanted to check off the items on your bucket list," he found himself explaining. "She wanted help and I figured I owed her so I volunteered." But it had been more than that. He just wasn't sure how much more.

Kade made a choking noise. "Really? She wanted to do the list for me?"

"You bet."

"I cribbed that list from the Internet," Kade said dryly. "Because she kept going on and on about how I needed some kind of goal for myself after I got out of the military."

Tye hadn't realized that Kade had decided months ago not to re-enlist. He filed that away to think about later.

"You stole the entire thing?"

Kade flashed Tye a look. "Except for the ménage part. I added that all on my own. Plus, I figured it'd shut her up."

"Hence the number two pole position."

"Yep."

"And you and Katie are really not—" He had to ask, had to know. If Kade still wanted a shot, he damned well deserved it.

"We broke up. Hell, we weren't ever really *together*." Kade sighed. "Being with Katie would have been good, but she deserved great."

"So it's true?"

"You should be asking Katie that."

"I did." He tossed his empty towards the milk crate full of recycling. "But I need to hear what you have to say."

"We're friends. We're always going to be. But anything else? That's over."

Tye could read between the lines. Kade and Katie had been lovers. His friend and teammate had held Katie in his arms, kissed her and loved on her. He wasn't sure how he felt about that, but he was sure it didn't matter. The past was the past. Mostly, he was glad Katie had had someone to love her. She deserved that.

"So." Kade curled his fingers around his beer can. "About you and my Katie."

"You just said she wasn't yours."

"Yeah, well—I lied. She's always going to be *mine*. I'm just considering sharing her with you. This is the part of the conversation where you man up and tell me what your intentions are."

Tye eyed his friend. "You really don't have any?"

Please tell me you don't.

Kade narrowed his eyes. "This isn't about me. It's about you. We already covered that."

Discussing his *feelings* for Katie ranked slightly higher on his fun list than, say, a root canal without a shot of Novocain. Too bad there wasn't a local anesthetic for the heart.

"She doing okay?"

"Damn it, man. What do you think?"

Tye didn't know. That was why he was asking. Katie deserved happy. Sure, the idea of *happy* having her wrapped up in Kade's arms made him want to holler and hit something, but the important factor in this equation was Katie. He wanted her smiling, no matter what it took.

"I'm not the guy who walked away from a woman like Katie," Kade said pointedly, when Tye didn't answer. "And thanks for me feeling like the girl in this relationship, discussing her feelings. Katie wanted *you*, dickhead. And you walked away from her."

Tye thought about that for a moment.

"Wanted or wants?" he asked. He snuck a peek at his watch. If he got his ass in gear, he could be sitting on Katie's front porch in under twenty minutes.

Kade sighed. "It's probably *wants*, but if you quote me on that, I'll have to kill you. You should tell her you love her. Just put it out there and see what she says."

"Got it." Tye stood up. He wasn't practicing his *I love you*s on Kade. Friendship only went so far.

Kade looked down. "Nice shoes."

The boots were fantastic, and only partly because they were a gift from Katie. She'd sent him a pair of boots. By the U.S. Post Office. The boots were something she'd labeled *chocolate brown* and softer than anything he'd ever owned. There was some kind of scroll-y design on the side, but his jeans covered that bit, so no worries. He wondered if she really took issue with his minimal shoe count or if she'd just been thinking about him.

"Katie took issue with my only owning three pairs of shoes," he said. Damned nice, too, although he was probably lucky his new boots weren't pink or decorated with ribbons.

"Tye?"

"Yeah?" He fished in his pocket for the keys to his truck. He could be at Katie's place in ten minutes.

"She's not home." Kade didn't bother trying to his grin. "She told me she was going hiking today."

"You know where?"

Kade waved a hand toward the ridge. "Up to the lookout on Black Ridge trail."

Tye frowned. "Jack was worried about that area. Said he might have spotted a sleeper smoke there, but he wasn't sure. Could have been someone's barbecue gone bad."

Automatically, they both looked towards the ridge. A puff of black smoke mushroomed over the treetops.

"Huh," Kade said. "That wasn't there an hour ago. That's no barbecue."

Tye didn't answer, because he was already racing for his truck.

CHAPTER SIXTEEN

Katie stopped and dropped when she hit the top of the trailhead. Her calves burned, she had to pee, and the view was spectacular. That made her one for three by her count. When she'd parked her Kia by the trailhead two hours ago, she'd planned on a nice, leisurely hike. Since she apparently didn't need to run a marathon after all, taking it easy was fine. Maybe she could also get some things straight in her head. Or walk long enough that the tired took over and her brain shut off.

She'd grabbed a couple of water bottles and her small pack with a bonus long-sleeved shirt because Kade had always insisted she travel with enough safety crap to play survivalist for a week, her sketchbook and some pencils and headed out. The first three miles, she set a nice, easy pace, focused on stretching out the kinks. Then she'd made the one-mile scramble up to the lookout point and broken out the emergency rations. Since her choices were a flattened PB&J and an oatmeal chocolate chip cookie the size of her hand, she liked to think she had her priorities straight. She went straight for the sugar.

While she munched, she stared out at the view. The Donovans' base camp was about fifteen miles southwest, below a neighboring ridge. Imagining Tye there, going about his day, was all too easy. And stupid. Whatever they'd had going on between them was over. He might be there checking gear or working out with the guys or doing any one of a dozen things that didn't involve her. At all. Unfortunately, she didn't seem to have gotten that memo.

She liked him. He was stubborn and opinionated and didn't talk much, if at all. But his eyes said things and the way he touched her, all rough-gentle... yeah, she liked that too. She also appreciated his easy acceptance of her need to honor Kade's wish list too. He had to be the only person who hadn't told her she was crazy. Except for the sharks. He really, really hadn't been on board with that part of the plan. She could feel the grin tugging at her face. *Bad grin.* They were over.

Completely, totally, until-hell-froze-over *over.*

Too bad turning her love for her bad-ass SEAL off wasn't anywhere near as easy as turning a faucet on and off. In fact, she had a bad feeling she might not be *able* to turn her feelings for Tye off.

Merde.

She polished off the cookie and stared at the horizon. Which was why she noticed when the chopper went up. The Donovans ran a tight ship, with plenty of practice drills. She watched for a minute, but the chopper didn't circle back over the base camp and unload jumpers. Instead, the bird headed in her general direction, before veering off and passing slightly southwest of her.

Falling for Tye Callahan would be a mistake. He'd made it perfectly clear that he was just passing through. Strong was a pit stop for him, but she'd made her home here. He also had that whole no emotions thing going on for him. For the most part, when it wasn't pitch black and he wasn't in the throes of a nightmare, Tye didn't like discussing feelings. Or admitting that he had them at all. How could she even begin to imagine long-term with someone like that?

Unfortunately, she could. All too easily.

The wind had picked up in the last half hour, and a steady breeze kept her vantage point on the rocks from becoming too hot. She tilted her sweaty face into the cool air, and plotted her next steps. All she needed now was a pool and a bikini. And a hot cabana boy. Unfortunately, none of those items were available on this particular mountainside, just the small, rather scummy pond downhill from the lookout point. It was no four-star swimming pool, though, and she'd turn green at the very least if she went in.

Something tickled her throat and she coughed. *Smoke*. There was a burn ban for all park areas because of the summer's dry conditions. Smoke had no business being out here.

She turned around and the reason for the chopper going airborne became painfully clear. Mother Nature had pulled a Dr. Jekyll and Mr. Hyde on her while she navel-gazed and mainlined cookie. The air on the other side of the ridge had smoked up, like a really bad smog day, a brownish film obscuring the view. *Smoke.*

The mountain was on fire.

She'd read Smokey the Bear posters. She'd dated Kade. But, while he'd certainly talked about his job and she'd listened, she hadn't taken notes. Or planned on reliving firsthand any of the fire scenarios he'd narrated. *Merde.* She'd signed the trailhead registry. Park service would know she was here and come looking for her. Right?

A puff of smoke, bigger, darker, *hungrier* shot up over the ridge and a small, glowing orange spark landed on the ground next to her.

Katie had hiked up to Black Ridge. When she hit the top, Tye told himself, she'd see the fire. Then, she'd have two choices: to head back down the way she'd come, or try the descending trail on the other side. The one that led straight into the fire. She was one of the smartest women he knew. She wouldn't go that way. The unwelcome voice in his head, however, reminded him that sometimes smart people did stupid things. They froze when they should act. They ran towards danger instead of away from it.

He pressed his foot down hard on the accelerator. Just in case. He'd be there for her just in case.

The closer he got to the trailhead, however, the more concerned he got. The afternoon winds had kicked in strong, and embers from the fire's frontline some miles away had ignited spot fires that blazed out of control. The last half mile, small patches of flame burned on both sides of the highway and everything kept getting darker overhead. It was like marching into Dante's Inferno. If she'd come up this way, however, she wasn't getting back down until the fire had passed over.

He pulled over at the trailhead, parking his truck in an empty spot next to Katie's Kia. Four minutes to unroll the portable aluminum fire shield over both vehicles—because there was every chance they'd need a speedy getaway once they got down the trail—and then he was reading the trailhead register, checking her entry time. She'd been gone three hours. She had to still be at the top.

After a quick radio call to Jack, to give the man a heads-up Tye was going in, he hit the trail.

Four miles to the lookout point Katie loved, according to Kade.

Dear God. *Let her be there.*

The wind had picked up, lifting burning debris up into the air and moving it along. The fastest he'd ever heard of a crown fire moving was nineteen miles-per-hour, but a quarter of a mile was more typical. Tye eyed the treetops. Nope. There was nothing typical about today's fire. The flames were moving like a fucking freight train, spurred on by the winds, and the fire line was likely no more than five or six miles away now.

And moving fast. Really, really fast.

The radio was crackling, spitting updates he didn't need because he had a front row seat.

Hooyah. Shit storm ahead.

Fire traveled faster uphill than down. Katie also needed to move in the opposite direction of the wind. Right now. A spark floated lazily past her in the air, the orange bead looking deceptively pretty and slow moving. She could hear Kade's lazy drawl in her head: if you see sparks in the air or hear cracking sounds, your ass is about to star front and center in a barbecue. It was too late to run. Based on what Kade had drummed into her head, the fire had to be less than a mile from her and people simply didn't outrun forest fires.

She cast a look at the path she'd hiked up so recently. Maybe... no. Dying wasn't part of her plans. All she had to do was keep her head and make good choices. It would be okay.

Unfortunately, her heart didn't buy the power of positive thinking, hammering hard enough that the panicked thunka-thunk drummed in her ears. Grabbing her pack, she started moving. The air over the fire was brown from the smoke and, even without her body's best efforts to hyperventilate, it was already much, much harder to breathe and see. She felt like she was stepping through insta-twilight despite the fact it was only afternoon.

The scummy pond looked damned good to her now.

She headed down the cutaway from the trail towards the pond, looking over her shoulder as she went. Doing this *definitely* wasn't on her bucket list. Maybe she had enough time to make it back to the trailhead and her Kia. Maybe the roads weren't blocked.

Maybe wasn't good enough.

She hit the edge of the pond and hesitated. Shoes on? Off? Was she over-reacting? Was there another way?

"Keep moving." The raspy, familiar voice made her shriek and whirl. Tye strode out of the pall of smoke seeping down the cutaway. Instead of his usual BDUs, he'd dressed for today's conditions in khaki workpants and a yellow Nomex shirt. She recognized the hardhat and pack from the hotshot crew that visited Strong for R&R, but the sunglasses and steel-toed work boots were all original Tye. She wasn't sure why she'd expected him to rappel into her hidey-hole wearing camo and a sniper rifle, but she had. Maybe that was just wishful thinking or just a flat-out bad idea. She was full of those today because right now she was wishing with everything she had that hiking had never even crossed her mind. After today, she was never leaving her couch. Or her house.

"Go," he said, but she waited for him to draw even with her anyhow.

"You're here," she said. Something flashed in her eyes. Surprise? Tye didn't know and now wasn't the time to find out. He'd gone after her because Kade couldn't on that bum leg of his. And because Tye would always come for her. No pun intended.

He shucked his work shirt and reached for her elbow, urging her into the water. She wasn't dressed for the firestorm bearing down on them. She wore cut-off jean shorts, a fire department T-shirt, and a pair of hiking boots with hot pink laces. He'd definitely found his Katie.

She splashed into the water. "Are you on a mission?"

His hands steadied her when she stumbled a little, the water sucking at her boots. "You bet."

She raised a brow.

"You," he whispered roughly against her ear. "You're my mission."

She opened her mouth. Closed it. Looked down at the pond water lapping around her knees as she slogged forward.

"We're going to play this safe," he said. "We've got a crown fire and a fireline moving in fast. There's no time to run, so if you're wearing anything made out of synthetic fabric, strip. Fast."

"What you see is what you get."

He checked the tag on her shirt. God bless the fire department for all-American one hundred percent cotton, and the jean shorts should be okay. "What do you have on underneath?"

"That's one hell of a pick-up line."

"Bra?" he asked impatiently. He estimated they had maybe ten minutes before they found out just how good their survival skills were. "If it's as pretty as the other ones I've seen, you need to take it off now. The fire should pretty much pass over us in the middle of the pond, but if the heat gets bad, it'll melt anything synthetic into your skin."

She shuddered and thrust her pack into his hand.

"Keep moving," he said. "Right to the center." He added her pack to his, and drew her forward. She shimmied in an endearingly awkward move, yanking the T-shirt up to her neck and shucking the prettiest purple bra he'd seen in a long time. Grabbing the lacy scrap, he shoved it into his pack. It should be fine there and, if it wasn't, then they wouldn't be in any condition to worry about it.

The water got deeper and the mission suddenly looked more like a sure thing. Katie floated, breast stroking ahead him.

He paused and held up her pack. "This waterproof?"

She looked back and shook her head. He eyed the ridge. He'd make it. Popping open the pack, he took a quick look. Most of the stuff didn't matter, but her sketchbook wasn't going to like the submersion. He transferred it to the waterproof pouch inside his own pack and then followed her to the center of the pond. The muddy bottom sucked at his boots, weighing him down. Unlike Katie, he had just enough height to keep his head clear.

"Hold onto me," he said and she did, her body brushing his. "I'll hold right back as soon as I've got us covered," he promised.

Moving quickly now, he popped the fire shelter out of his pack and yanked it over their heads as best he could, pulling his Nomex shirt over Katie's head, creating a little igloo. He pulled her wet T-shirt up over her nose and mouth. Two layers had to be enough. It was cooler and darker beneath the shelter, but not by much.

"Face as close to the water as you can," he ordered and her hands tightened around his waist. He scooped her closer, turning her so he had his back between her and the flames. The air heated up as the wall of flame moved closer and closer, lighting up their sanctuary. It sounded like a freight train bearing down on them.

"Don't run," he said. "Don't panic. Thirty seconds. Maybe twice that. And then it's over. If it gets really bad, I'm going to push you under."

"That's a lot of orders," she said weakly. "And we both know I'm no good at taking orders."

"Make an exception," he suggested. She rested her head on his chest. He could touch the bottom, but she was too short. That was okay by him. He liked holding her. "I won't let anything bad happen to you."

"Only good things?"

"I promise."

She was silent for a moment. He rested his head on top of hers, drinking her in as he ran through the logistics of their escape in his head. He'd done everything could. All that was left was the waiting, praying and holding on. Funny how it all seemed better when he was doing his waiting with Katie in his arms.

"Tye?"

"Right here."

"I don't have a bucket list. It might not matter—" The catch in her voice had something long forgotten inside him turning over.

"It will," he said fiercely. "You have my word on that, angel. What's on your list?"

"Bora Bora would be nice. Somewhere tropical and hot without the flames. I'd like to walk down the streets of Paris in a pair of five-inch Louboutins. And—" She hesitated.

The fire got louder. They were either almost out of time or they were about to start the rest of their lives.

"Yeah?" he prompted.

"I'd like to find the courage to speak my mind. To say what's in my heart."

"That's a good thing," he agreed, brushing his cheek against her T-shirt wrapped head. He shifted his hand, readying for the back-up plan. If he burned, he'd have just enough time to shove her under and pray she could hold her breath long enough.

"Okay." She sucked in a breath. "We might not have much time here, but I can knock that last one off my list."

"Angel—" The fire lit up their Nomex cave. *Show time.* He sank lower, cradling her tight.

"I love you, Tye Callahan."

He didn't know which hit him harder—the fire or her words.

The fire roared over them, around them. Sucking greedily at the air. The water heated up and it was bright as day beneath the shelter and his jacket. Hot and then hotter. Her heart pounded and all she could do was hold on and pray. She wanted to run. To scream. To *do* something, anything but wait. She'd spent a lifetime waiting and she was so, so done with it.

"Shhh," Tye said into her ear.

"Talk to me?" she gasped out. She couldn't *do* this and yet the alternative was too awful to contemplate.

"Thirty seconds," he said. "Thirty, twenty-nine, twenty-eight..."

He counted down the seconds in a rough whisper, his voice a welcoming beacon in all that heat.

At seven the heat dropped abruptly and the light died down.

At zero, he stopped and listened. "I'm going to check it out. You're going to submerge for the count of five while I look. If we're all clear, I'll tap your shoulder, you'll come up, and we'll move out."

"Why?"

"Orders," he said quietly. "I'm looking. You're waiting. That's how this is going to work."

She wanted to argue, but it was a battle she wouldn't win. Instead, she sank below the surface, his hand pressing down gently on her head, not taking chances. Three long seconds later, he moved his hand, tapped her shoulder, and she shot to the surface.

Twenty minutes after that, they were back on the trail, moving silently and quickly towards the parking lot. Katie still couldn't believe how much those thirty seconds underneath the fire shelter had changed the world. Gone were the leafy green treetops and the dense undergrowth. Instead, crayon-orange flames licked up the tree trunks and little was left in the way of green stuff on the forest floor.

To her surprise, her Kia was fine. Not only had the fire not reached that section of the highway, but a shiny space-age blanket was layered over her car. She shot Tye a glance as he started pulling the shield off with his work gloves.

"You gift-wrapped my car."

He grimaced. "I probably should have let it burn so you could collect on the insurance."

Two hundred yards up the road, a column of super-heated flame rose overhead, debris shooting off like bottle rockets and snaking through the air. What had been a normal trail, an everyday highway was now an inferno. Although the asphalt itself wasn't burning, everything on the southern side of the road was. Backlit by the blaze, two hundred foot pines went up in flames, adding more black smoke to the darkened sky as fire laddered up the trunks and headed for the dry canopy up top.

"So," she said, fishing in her damp backpack for her keys. What did you say after a guy risked his life to come after you? She didn't want to imagine hunkering down in that pond without him.

"You okay to drive?" he asked, ever practical. "It's not too late to leave your car here and ride back with me."

She shook her head. "I can't chance it."

"Right." He opened her door for her. Shut it. Waited for something.

Merde. She had no idea what he was thinking.

Instead of trying to figure it out—because she'd already proved singularly bad at *that*—she turned the key in the ignition and got the Kia started. Tye tapped on the window.

"I'll follow you back," he said when she rolled the window down.

"Okay," she agreed, wanting to reach out and drag him into the car. To say *something*, anything. Instead, she settled for, "Thank you."

Maybe Hallmark made cards commemorating the saving of one's ass by a fireman hottie.

He reached out and ran a thumb down her cheek. "Anytime, angel. Roll the window up in case you hit smoke."

He turned and walked back to his truck, so she got going.

The way back home had changed every bit as much as the trail. Cows wandered through burned out sections of forest, wisps of white smoke curling around the bases of the trees. Katie could almost pretend it was fog, except the trunks were blackened and the lower branches curled up from the heat. The cows looked good though, avoiding the occasional spot fire.

When she got to her bungalow, though, Tye flashed his blinkers and kept on driving.

CHAPTER SEVENTEEN

Finding Katie ass-deep in fire had taken ten years off his life. Maybe twenty. Tye didn't know which, just that she'd scared the hell out of him and he didn't know what to do with the fear. He'd pulled her into the pond and then he'd marched her back down the mountain. Seen her home.

And kept on driving.

The whole time, however, her words had rung in his ears. *I have a bucket list. I love you.*

He hadn't known what to say. Or, rather, he'd known what he wanted to say—*I love you too*—but the words had got stuck in his throat and there'd been a goddamned forest fire bearing down on them, so her timing sucked. So he'd kept on driving, while he thought things out, and then he'd got to his camper and everything had been suddenly, perfectly clear. He didn't belong *there*. He belonged with Katie. Wherever that was. So he'd called Kade, hitched the camper to the truck and moved out.

This time, when he pulled up in front of her bungalow, she was parked in the double swing on the front porch. She had her usual empty spot beside her, the one he'd assumed would be reserved for Kade.

He was all in. If she threw in her cards, he'd have to come up with another plan, but for now he was flying on a hope and a prayer. She watched him maneuver the camper rig into a neat parallel parking job in front of her place and the place was total Americana, right down to the yellow roses blooming by the porch. Strong and Katie were a far cry from Khost. But it could be home. He held onto that thought like a lifeline. The nuts and bolts of his parking job only occupied thirty seconds, and then he was out of excuses.

He got out of the truck, turned and faced the porch. And the woman who had no idea she held his goddamned heart in her hands.

Curled up on the swing, surrounded by mismatched pillows and potted ferns, Katie belonged there one hundred percent. He almost looked behind him for a husband coming up the drive with a couple of kids in tow. And possibly a pet or two or three. His heart squeezed. This was why coming out here had been a bad idea. He had more than enough money to give her the house and the animals, but he didn't know if he was capable of the emotions that went with those things and made them more than *things*.

Made them a life.

She watched him come, kicking her foot back and forth. She was barefoot again, he noticed, her shoes kicked off on the porch's wood planks.

"Hey," he said, when he got close.

"Hey yourself." She didn't move, but she seemed unsurprised to see him. Probably Kade had warned her he was coming. It was good she had someone watching her back. Not that she needed looking out for, but he liked the idea that someone who cared for her was keeping an eye out.

He reached a hand out and pulled her foot to a slow halt. "Is there room for two?"

She slid over without answering and he dropped onto the seat beside her. The padded cushions were still warm from her body, and he took a moment to just enjoy being where she'd been. He'd take what he could get, because he had no idea how this conversation was going to go.

"You came home," he said and wanted to smack himself.

Hell. That was obvious, which made him three kinds of an idiot, because where else would she have gone? He'd *watched* her turn into the driveway. He didn't know what had been said between her and Kade since Kade's return, but Kade had made it clear that the two of them weren't a romantic item. Thank God. And Tye hadn't asked her to stay.

He should have.

He knew that now.

But instead of putting the words out there, he stared. Christ, she looked good. Her tank top was casual and looked comfortable. Nothing fancy, but so damned beautiful, like Katie herself. The straps framed the strong lines of her collarbones and the golden brown skin he'd kissed. He wanted to bury his face in the crook of her neck and kiss her some more.

He definitely should have told her how he felt.

"I have a job here," she reminded him.

Right. The art lessons. He probably shouldn't be jealous of a bunch of five-year-olds and geriatrics.

She pushed off with her foot, setting the swing into motion again. The going was slower and harder with him on board, but she clearly was itching to move. For a long moment, he worked the swing with her, enjoying the contrast of his steel-toe next to her bare foot. He was all large and rough where she was feminine and delicate. And, fuck, he didn't know when he'd started thinking in poetry.

Get the words out. Surely, if he could think them, he could say them.

Nope.

He was an idiot.

He didn't deserve a second chance. Coming here wasn't fair to her, not if she was putting her life back together. Whatever had happened between them before Kade had come home was part of the past.

"You look good," he said finally, when it became clear she wasn't going to break the silence. In some ways, though, that silence felt right. It was okay to not talk, to just sit and swing. Another day, he'd have enjoyed the sensation. Today, however, there was something he still needed to say.

"Are you leaving?" The question was straightforward, but her eyes hinted at other emotions. Humor? Sadness? Maybe a little of both, although his ability to read her had proved faulty in the past. Fuck it. He didn't like this distance between them. He moved closer, his shoulder bumping hers, erasing the careful inches she'd put between them.

He'd come here determined to put everything on the line. To put himself out there and, yeah, beg her to take him.

"I wanted to tell you something," he said roughly.

"Uh-huh."

Katie's fingers walked up his chest, and he should have warned her that touching him now was like playing with fire, but damn it, he wanted her hands on him.

"Yeah." He closed his arms around her, holding her tight. When he rubbed a hand over her back, he could feel the fragile curve of her spine, but there was nothing fragile about this woman. She was tough.

"Tye?" Katie tilted her head back until she could see his eyes. The look on her face was a mix of sympathy and determination. Yeah. She'd take no for an answer, but then this time when she walked she'd do it alone, and she wouldn't be coming back. If he wanted any chance with her, he had to find the words he'd been avoiding.

Her arms tightened around him, and he wondered who was holding who.

"Past tense?" Her soft question got right to the heart of the matter. "*Wanted* instead of *want?*"

"With you, it's always *want*. I don't see that changing."

"*Oui*," she breathed out, but that was all.

The swing went forward and backward, and for the longest time they sat, watching night creep in around the house. Mountain nights weren't afraid to speak up, and the crickets shrilled louder and louder as the dark grew. A train whistle moaned, passing through in the distance, and the toads called back and forth, hunting for mates and sex. Katie snuck peeks at Tye's face, hard but not so distant now, because he'd been hurt but he'd opened up anyway. Instead of launching into words, she focused on breathing.

Which didn't help. He smelled good, in a way that made her heart squeeze with recognition. Soap and outdoors and hot, hard male. She inhaled again, storing up memories. Too bad she couldn't bottle him up and bring him out in the years to come, because there were no guarantees she'd get to keep him. Maybe he'd come back, do another summer in Strong, but those were *maybes*. Not *definites*.

And yet here he was.

With his camper hitched to the back of his truck.

She didn't know what to think, but getting her hopes up was a good way to get her heart broken, and she'd had enough pain this month, thank you very much. So she swung and settled and waited.

Eventually, however, his thumb nudged her face up. "Are we okay?"

Giving in to temptation, she leaned into him and met his gaze. The look in his eyes was unfamiliar, full of something she hadn't seen there before. Or maybe it had been there, and she simply hadn't recognized it. It didn't matter. All that counted now was this moment and this man. It was time to take that leap of faith.

"Yes," she said softly. "We're okay, Tye."

"Promise?" He rubbed his thumb over her cheek, slow and steady.

"Are you worried?" She didn't know what he was asking. All she knew was that his question mattered. "What do you want from me?" She reminded herself to breathe. Maybe his question was nothing more than empty words, a polite sop before he drove off and left her here on her front porch.

"Everything. I want it all, Katie." He leaned over, shifting closer. "Every inch, every thought. Every night and every morning. Will you give me that?"

The dreamy slo-mo of the swing ceased, and her eyes stung. *Don't cry.* He was still new to this emotional-sharing thing, and she needed to break him in slowly. But there was a grin spreading across her face, she could feel it, and maybe that made up for the wet eyes.

"That's a tall order," she said.

"True," he whispered roughly. One booted foot planted on the porch, dragging the swing to a halt, and he pulled her onto his lap. Heat and his arms surrounded her. "But I'm thinking you could handle it, if I gave you the right incentive."

She wrapped her arms around his waist. "Which would be?"

"Myself. Which is," he admitted, "pretty damn self-serving of me. I want you to come back with me. Or I'll stay put here. We'll work something out."

"To Uncle Sam?"

"Wherever we decide to go. You've got me hard and fast, Katie, and I'm never getting clear. Hell," he whispered roughly, pressing a kiss against her forehead, "with you, I'm home and right where I want to be. Why would I fight it?"

"Why not?" He had to say it, she needed him to say it, because how often did a girl's secret fantasies come true while she was sitting on her front porch?

"Because I love you," he growled. "We'll go wherever you want. We can come back here if that's what you need, or we can just never leave." His eyes made heated promises, and summer spent in his arms sounded just about perfect. His next words were the icing on the cake. "Marry me, Katie Lawson, so we can do this for the rest of our lives."

Yes. Please.

"Besides, I need someone to help me with my bucket list." He fished a folded list out of his back pocket.

She took it and bit back a smile. He'd written a bucket list of things to do with *her*. The over-water bungalow in Bora Bora was definitely something she could get behind. Of course, the more she read, the bigger her grin got.

"Tye, half of these have to do with sex."

"Yeah." He grinned at her. "But only half. I have my priorities straight. You can get your swim with the shark fix in Bora Bora. On our honeymoon."

"You don't want to sit on my porch for the rest of our lives?" She laughed up at him, because it was that or shriek and cry.

He growled, "Come here, you," and covered her mouth with his.

His lips muffled her *I love you*, but that was okay. There was love and tenderness and laughter in their kiss, and they both knew it. Tye might always be a bad ass SEAL at heart, but now he was as much hers as she was his.

Forever.

Made in the USA
San Bernardino, CA
13 December 2016